"Surely you don't need to be introduced to my sister after all these years?" Hector teased with a hearty laugh that made Meg cringe.

She lifted her chin and looked Lord Clement in the eye, eager to get the greeting over and done with. "My lord."

Lord Clement's lips parted in obvious surprise. "Lady Margaret?"

"Meg," she said, nodding to him. "No one has called me by my full name since our mother passed."

Lord Clement shook his head suddenly. "Forgive me, but I would never have recognized you."

"I thought the same of you," she murmured, and then fidgeted under his startlingly direct gaze.

The characters and events portrayed in this book are fictitious. Any similarity to real persons, living or dead, is purely coincidental and not intended by the author.

HEATHER BOYD

USAT BESTSELLING AUTHOR

One
ENCHANTED
CHRISTMAS

Distinguished Rogues

13

Chapter One

Lady Meg Stockwick covered her cold nose and mouth again and blew out a breath, hoping to warm her face a little bit. Meg was not used to traveling in the winter months. She was not used to traveling at all really. She was doing her best not to become an icicle.

Her brother was to blame for her discomfort, not that he seemed to care.

Until recently, she'd never had reason to venture from the family home on the coast of Dorset. But it was Hector's home now; her brother had assumed control of their father's estate and title upon his death, and she was supposed to obey the new viscount—even if she couldn't seem to stop questioning his decisions.

"It's not too late to turn back," Meg told him urgently as Hector's new traveling chariot began the slow descent into yet another blindingly white valley. "We could be home by Christmas morning."

"It certainly is too late. We're almost there," her brother assured her as he scrubbed the damp from the window with his fist. "You will enjoy yourself."

Meg doubted that as she huddled more deeply into her coverings. The sun had come out to shine at last and brought with it Hector's enthusiasm for new surroundings. He had been saying she'd enjoy herself repeatedly for the last day, and she was still quite sure he was wrong. Spending the anniversary of the worst month of her life in Derbyshire, at the home of a terrible rogue, was not her idea of fun.

"We should still celebrate Christmas the way we always have," Meg insisted, determined to win her brother over. "In our home. I had everything in hand before you arrived."

"Next year you can do as you wish," he promised. "But this year I have other plans than sitting in Dorset all alone."

Meg shivered, wishing her brother had stayed in London. His return had heralded an upset of all her plans for the holidays. And now she was here, far from home and all she'd ever known. Meg had heard nothing good about her brother's closest friend in the past few years and now she would be forced into close proximity with him for weeks.

She had known Lord Clement as a boy, but it had been a decade since she'd lain eyes on him. She had heard enough to form a clear picture of his character though. Lord Clement was often gallivanting about London with her brother, too important to visit their little coastal village. Meg believed him to be a terrible influence on her older brother.

She heaved a heavy sigh. There was only one thing to look forward to this holiday. Lady Vyne, the rogue's mother, was certain to be better company. Lady Vyne had written Meg many comforting letters in recent years following the death of her mother and then her father so soon after.

Hector suddenly began gathering his possessions—book, handkerchief, and a pouch of sweet meats he'd procured along the way—and stuffed them into a leather satchel he'd kept at his side for the entire trip.

Meg hugged her book close to her chest. "Mother and Father are still with us in spirit," she argued.

Hector shifted forward to stare at her, his expression grave. "If Mother and Father are spirits as you continue to claim, and watching over us as well, then surely they've heard our itinerary many times from your own lips and will have hitched a ride."

Meg wished that might be so. Did ghosts

ever take a holiday? "That is how they met. Father climbed into the wrong carriage, and they fell in love."

"By the time they reached the fourth turnpike," Hector said softly.

"Love at first sight." Meg wanted so much to believe in the impossible right now. Even though she had Hector still, she felt very alone without her parents. There was no one to tell her secrets to and no one who gave her theirs to keep. Two years of death, first her mother and then her father, and the constant period of mourning had been hard to bear for everyone. Her closest friends had married and moved away to start new lives with their husbands already. She had lost touch with all but a few.

Hector had been away in London when their father had died, but he had rushed home to be with her for the burial. He had not stayed long, traveling back to London to meet with Lord Clement while she had mourned alone.

And now Hector insisted she must travel with him. In the winter!

"Cheer up, old thing," Hector said. "Who knows what might happen during the holidays."

Nothing good, she suspected. Not if Lord Clement was anywhere in the vicinity of her brother. She might not see much of Hector either. That was not how she wanted to see out the year.

Meg huddled farther beneath the warm furs, trying to resign herself to the fate her brother had forced upon her. "I'm still in mourning," she reminded him. "Even if you forbid me to be."

He shoved his satchel aside roughly. "It was past time!"

Meg glared at him. "Papa deserved to be mourned for a full year as we did with Mother. Six months is hardly long enough."

"Enough is enough," he cried, smacking his fist on his thigh. "You will do as I say, and be grateful I care enough to take you to visit my friends at all. I am the head of our family and you will enjoy yourself." Her brother scowled. "I insist you make merry."

Meg glared at him. "You cannot make me pretend."

Hector pinched the bridge of his nose, a sure sign she was trying his patience. "You will not embarrass me by spoiling Christmas for Lord Clement and me."

Meg pressed her lips together tightly, affronted that Hector thought more of Lord Clement's happiness than hers. "You don't seem to care what I want anymore," she grumbled even though knowing she was being difficult. This trip had been a tax on her nerves. She'd barely slept last night in yet another strange bed.

She slumped in her seat as her eyes pricked with the threat of tears. There were days she did not like her brother. He gambled away his fortune and spent far too many nights out in society. His improved situation had gone to his head. She'd also heard gossip he had a woman in London too—the sort Mama had whispered must never be acknowledged.

"I do care. Very much, and it is high time I did right by you and brought you out in society." Hector nodded. "Gentleman have to see you in order to ask to marry you."

Meg blushed at the idea of marrying a stranger. Hector was all for that. "You speak such nonsense. No one will notice me here."

"On the contrary, Lady Vyne is sure to host at least one dinner during our stay. There's a village not far from the manor house, too, and we will be here until after Twelfth Night don't forget. Anything can happen in that amount of time."

Meg turned up her nose. "That village has an alehouse, I assume?"

Hector grinned widely. "Every village tends to have at least one. Gentlemen come for miles around and some of them call on Lady Vyne, and Clement, too. They will assist with any introductions if they deem the connection suitable."

He had an answer for everything. "As if Lord Clement would stir himself on my behalf."

Hector chuckled. "He's a good friend."

"I thought I was that to you once," Meg grumbled.

"You're worse. You're my unmarried little sister. It is required that I adore you," Hector teased, grinning as he tapped her nose. "Even when you are out of sorts. If the signs of merriment bother you so much, just try not to scowl at everyone for the duration of our stay. Don't spoil Christmas for the rest of us. Mother and Father would hate to know you were so miserable."

She heaved a heavy sigh. Hector was probably right, but Mother and Father had made this time of year special. She had hoped to do the same but for Hector instead. "I will do my best. To honor their memory."

Hector turned his attention back to the view. "Excellent."

Meg glanced out the foggy windowpane, too. It wasn't Hector's way to let grief smother his good spirits. He had lived away from home for a long time. He'd not borne the worry of caring for either of their parents as they had declined.

He meant this trip as a way to end their mourning.

Meg might never end hers, no matter what happened. Her life had not been the same since her mother and then her father had passed, and it could never improve.

Frustrated that her breath had fogged the window again, she rubbed a circle on the pane with her fist and glared at the rolling fields of white powder until she realized she was looking down at their destination.

The manor on The Vynes estate, a widespread yellow stone structure, sat at the end of a long, winding road. Snowy mounds hiding what might be garden shrubbery dotted the landscape, bordered by low stone walls around the dwelling. But everything that could be pretty or green was hidden beneath inches of snow. There was no warmth here.

Meg desperately missed the rolling blue of the sea and the sound of crashing waves upon the shore near her home. It had been three days since she'd been bundled into this carriage, and two uncomfortable nights sleeping at posting houses along the way.

She focused her gaze back on the nearing house with a sense of foreboding. The family they were visiting were a good bit wealthier than they were, and it was a larger family, too. Lord Clement had a mother and father, Lord and Lady Vyne, a younger pair of unmarried sisters, and an infant brother as well. It was going to be a noisy few weeks in the country, and awkward to be with another family.

But Hector grinned as the carriage began to travel around the circular drive that would bring them to a stop before an impressive pair of oak doors. "Ready to dash inside and begin to make merry?"

"If my legs haven't gone numb yet." She smiled with false brightness. "As ready as I'll ever be."

But there was little chance this was going to be a happy Christmas. Meg was sure it might just be the worst ever.

Chapter Two

Otis considered the cards dealt him and then placed them face down on the comforter. "Your hand."

His father, the seventh Earl of Vyne, smirked as he drew the winnings across the bed. Father didn't even try to hide his glee anymore when he won the games they played— even when it was just a few pounds. "As always, Clement."

If only Vyne knew the truth of the matter. Otis played the part of a dutiful son but he kept his feelings about gambling and his father's lucky streaks strictly to himself. Otis was an expert card player. He could win the hands that mattered and lose others at will. But Father's health was declining rapidly, so Otis chose to let him feel lucky at least in this. "Another game?"

Father considered the suggestion, long and hard, and then shook his gray head. "I've reclaimed enough of my rightful inheritance back from you for one day."

Otis' inheritance, left to him by his grandfather in an unbreakable will, was a continual source of friction between them. Father had been unable to successfully challenge it, and he'd been furious with Otis ever since.

The fact that Otis' personal fortune now exceeded all expectations was unforgivable to Vyne. The earl had expected that money to be his upon the last earl's demise, and went out of his way to try to get every penny back.

Otis only played against Father, and lost often, so he might not be expelled from The Vynes again. He'd been banished to London for six months after the reading of the will. In that time, Father had made Mother's life hell, blaming her for everything and anything he did not like. For Mother's sake, and the happiness of his siblings, Otis had pledged to dower his sisters and committed additional funds to his younger brother's education.

Those small measures were all the concessions Grandfather's will had allowed Otis to make. He could give nothing to his father outright even if he had wanted to.

However, making those small commitments had been enough to be forgiven a little and allowed to return to the home he loved more than any other place in England.

Otis wished to keep a close eye on his siblings, and his mother, too. Mother was forbidden to leave the estate now, and so were the children. Father controlled everyone else here, even from the sick room, with an iron fist. Otis would gladly lose a little more money every now and then to keep the tyrant happy. "What shall we do then?"

Father's eyes narrowed. "I've been thinking about family."

Otis kept his face impassive as he waited for him to continue. Family was a topic that interested him greatly.

Father sat back, one thumb poised on the tip of his chin. "You do not ask the direction my thoughts have traveled, my son?"

The last time they had talked of "family" a sister's marriage had been arranged out of the blue in a fit of spite. Thankfully, the groom had been a decent enough fellow and had met with his sister's approval in the end. "Yes, of course I do."

"You must marry."

So Father had finally broached the subject Otis had been expecting for some time. Otis was already prepared. "I know."

Otis was six and twenty. Father was four and fifty. Mortality had become Father's greatest fear in recent years. "The succession must continue without interruption," Father announced pompously. "Unless you intend for your brother to inherit the estate."

Otis' brother was still a babe really. "I said I *will* marry."

"I want you settled before the season has begun," Lord Vyne insisted.

Otis sat back in his chair—stunned by the rush but unwilling to show it. "Wouldn't it be simpler for me to head to London for the season and choose from the cream of the crop?"

Father's expression grew sly. "My son has no reason to compete with the rabble of society. Not when I already have a well-dowered filly picked out for him."

Father believed that Otis shared his taste in women. Otis had quickly learned to play into that delusion over the years, but he would not when it came to choosing a wife. "I've no intention of competing with anyone. The ladies would be coming to me, not I to them, I'm sure."

Father grunted in agreement. "Be that as it may, I have taken it upon myself to issue an invitation for the holiday. My acquaintance has a suitable daughter in need of a husband. The family lacks a title but the girl's dowry is appropriately large. You will find her to your liking."

Good grief, Father was well advanced with this scheme. Even from bed he would try to direct Otis' life. Father had a number of friends. Otis loathed each and every one of them. Marrying one of their daughters was not in his best interests. "What is the chit's name?"

"Does it matter?"

Otis winced. He held women in the highest regard, while his father did not. "It does if I need to address her."

Father sat back with a sigh. "One of Milne's girls."

Milne was probably the best of the bunch. New money. Ambitious. Someone Otis had never truly warmed to though. Otis had honestly expected Father to suggest some duke's younger daughter or a widowed countess as his wife. The Milne chit he'd met was pretty, intelligent, but there were a few complications attached to her that did not suit Otis at all. "I think I recall meeting one. Dark hair, brown eyes. She had a fondness for yapping terriers if I recall correctly."

Otis was allergic to dogs, and Father knew it.

He frowned for a moment and then nodded. "If she is to be your countess, she must give up her small companions," Father decreed.

"Hardly kind."

"Only a fool pays attention to what a woman wants," Father claimed.

Otis was probably a fool then in Father's estimation. He stood, aiming to appear nonchalant, but his mind was racing as he took a few steps away from the bed toward the tall windows. He would not agree to marry just anyone Father chose. He may not know what exactly he wanted in a wife but possessing a large dowry held no lure for him.

Otis glanced out the window and caught sight of an unfamiliar traveling chariot pulling up before the manor. *Blast*. Was that the Milnes arriving already?

If so, Otis had little time to come up with a plan to turn them aside. Since Father's bed was too far away from the window to notice his guests had arrived yet, there was a chance Otis could pretend he hadn't, either.

As much as he was loath to leave the estate so suddenly, retreat might be his best option for the immediate future. He needed time to think of whom he might make a match with. If he could name a worthy alternative, he might yet have his way without too much of a struggle. He could leave for a day or two, avoid the Milnes, while he considered his options. Mother would understand his absence if he explained his reasons for going.

"I suggest you win Milne over first. I wager The Vynes you'll have a bride in hand before Christmas Day arrives."

Father's propensity for making wagers was why Grandfather had skipped over his eldest son in favor of leaving everything not entailed to a grandson—to Otis. Grandfather had valued Otis' intelligence and believed he would protect the family from the worst of Vyne's excesses. "This is not a decision I can make without due consideration."

"That is why they are coming to visit," Father insisted. "You will get to know one another very well indeed in the next days. If you are still unsure, test her mettle in the bedchamber if you must."

Otis stilled, disturbed by Father's suggestion. "I will do no such thing."

"Do you require further incentive to do as duty requires?" Father's eyes narrowed.

Just how low could Father get? "What are you suggesting?"

"As a reward for taking a bride, you may take your mother to the seaside for the summer," Father offered.

Father wielded absolute control over his family. He must want this alliance very badly indeed. "Mother would enjoy that, but only if the children could join her there, too."

It was a lot to hope for, but the more Otis

considered the prize of the wager, Mother's freedom, the more he warmed to the idea of making such a deal. But only if the circumstances could be in his favor, too. Otis knew the Milne girl only a little and had never considered her in the role of wife before. Bedding a wife before any wedding, while reprehensible the way Father described it, might have been possible if they liked each other and he'd proposed first.

But a few days was not enough time in his opinion to decide on a bride, even if this was a chance to help his mother escape Father's control. If he pretended to consider Miss Milne and could prove she did not suit him, or the family, he would be free to choose another later. But he needed time for that.

"I'll take that wager," Otis said slowly. "On the condition that I am allowed an appropriate length of time for a proper courtship before any marriage takes place."

"What do you need to court her for? Just wed her and be done with it."

"No. I must know that the lady I marry feels more affection for me than my title."

Father snorted. "Engage a mistress and you will have a surfeit of attention."

"Mistresses love money, not the men they bed." He pursed his lips, disliking this discussion immensely. "Those are my terms."

"Don't be difficult about this."

"I have made a reasonable request so I may choose the best candidate to become a countess one day. The honor of the family demands it." Otis raised one brow. "Are you afraid that time will prove you've misjudged Miss Milne's suitability?"

Father glared. "Her dowry alone is worth the inconvenience of making a match without affection."

"Not to me." Otis shrugged. "But there's always London in the new year."

"No. You will wed Miss Milne. You have until Twelfth Night to propose."

Otis would not risk his own chance at happiness. "It cannot be done."

Father never liked to compromise, and his eyes narrowed. "You will court her."

"I can, but I make no promises about proposing."

Father stared at him. "Let me put it this way—if you fail to marry within three months, you'll never set foot here again until I'm dead."

Otis straightened. "No!"

Father smirked. "Exile, or a marriage in three months so you can take your mother and siblings away for as long as you'd like?"

Otis was thunderstruck. The price of failure was too bloody high.

Father extended his hand, his eyes alight

with glee as he waited for Otis to accept his final terms. "Which is it to be?"

Otis, however, strode to the door and yanked it open. The footman jumped back at least a foot. "Fetch witnesses."

Father had never reneged on a bet, but there was always a first time. There must be written proof to ensure Mother could leave the estate when Otis tied the knot. Otis wouldn't hesitate to blackmail Father with it to get his way, if necessary.

When the steward entered, Otis explained what he wanted written down. The steward was pale by the end, but Otis asked for two copies to be made of the original. They signed all of them, and Otis tucked his copy into his pocket for safekeeping.

Thankfully, Father was so confident of winning that he never noticed the omission of Miss Milne's name in the terms of the wager. Otis was still free to marry anyone he chose, and still win that bet, but he only had three months to do it. Since that was the case, he would be heading to London after the holiday. Unfortunately, that meant he would have to meet with Miss Milne first.

He folded the last copy in half and handed it to the steward. "Keep that somewhere safe."

The steward knew Father well enough that Otis did not have to say to keep evidence of the wager anywhere Father could not get his hands on it. The man backed from the chamber with a deep bow and fled quickly.

Otis glanced out the window again, noting the carriage was drawing away toward the stables. Milne and his daughters must be in the drawing room with Mother by now.

He turned to his father. "Wasn't one of Milne's girls going to marry Lord Bellows?"

Father sneered. "I wager Milne would not allow his blood to mingle with that of a known imbecile, even if he *is* an earl."

"Is that right?" Otis nodded along, but disapproved of his father's attitude. Lord Bellows was not as smart as many people might want him to be. But he was genuine and a decent sort. Otis had thought it a smart match for the Bellows line. Miss Milne seemed intelligent. "A pity. "I thought her very fond of the man. She could have discretely guided Bellows, for the benefit of all involved. When might we expect the Milnes to arrive?"

"Not for a few days yet."

"That's a shame," he murmured…but wondered who was in the drawing room now with Mother?

Otis let out a quiet sigh. He had a reprieve of a few days from Miss Milne. He hadn't a moment to lose getting his affairs in order before he made the journey to London though.

"I have to run a few errands. If you will excuse me, Father. I should be about my business."

"Yes, go, but make sure you are here when Milne arrives." Lord Vyne made an impatient gesture to dismiss Otis. "I promised the man an enjoyable holiday."

Otis fled. The Milnes were going to be disappointed.

Chapter Three

Meg did her best to curtsy to the Countess of Vyne despite her exhaustion. "Thank you for having us."

The countess drew close and placed her hands on Meg's frozen cheeks. "My dear, it is so good to see you again."

"The pleasure is ours," Meg assured her, trying not to shiver.

The countess impulsively embraced Meg then, enveloping her in sweet-smelling warmth. She drew back quickly and led Meg toward the great hearth where a large fire blazed. "Come to the fire and warm yourself. You look almost done for."

"No, I'm quite well," Meg promised, though she was eager for the warmth. She glanced back over her shoulder but her brother waved her away. "It is a bit colder than I'm used to."

"I know it is," the countess assured. The countess perched at her side. "I have looked forward to having you here since the day I read about your mother passing. I would have sent for you sooner if I thought you might have come."

"My father needed me," Meg murmured.

Father had taken the death of Meg's mother very badly indeed. He had only left the house to bury her, and then locked himself away from the world bereft of her vital presence. It had taken all of Meg's cunning to get him to eat, to sleep. He said he couldn't imagine a life without Mother and now he did not have to. Meg had done everything in her power to ease his mourning and it hadn't been enough. He'd slipped away a little more each day, until a sniff had become a cough, and then fever had set in despite her best efforts to have him cured.

"You did everything you could," the countess promised, and then smiled. "Now you are here, I am determined we will all have a lovely Christmas together. My daughters were particularly excited that you were coming, so too are the boys."

Not all the boys, surely.

Meg held her hands out to the flames and listened in silence as the countess described merriment that was planned for the coming weeks. The countess was enthusiastic but everything she mentioned reminded Meg of past Christmases with her parents, and that made her heart heavier.

She looked toward her brother just as a stranger rushed into the room. "What the devil are you doing here?"

"What do you mean? We were invited!" Hector exclaimed. "It's damn good to see you again, Clement."

Meg gaped, and then snapped her mouth shut. *That* was Lord Clement? She barely recognized him.

As a boy he'd been skinny with a shock of dark hair that he'd always been brushing from his eyes. Those longish locks were gone now, replaced by a shorter cropped style that revealed a pair of intelligent eyes set in an attractive face.

Meg glanced at Lady Vyne quickly, and discovered Lord Clement had grown up to resemble his mother. But he was far taller and broad shouldered than even her brother was. He was handsome now. More so than she'd ever imagined a man could be.

Lord Clement was unlike anything Meg was prepared to meet.

Meg averted her eyes as her cheeks suddenly heated.

But she couldn't help but peek again. Lord Clement and Hector embraced, shook hands vigorously, and expressed such joy to see each other that Meg immediately felt envious.

"And here I was merely hoping you would write me a letter before New Year," Lord Clement exclaimed.

"Well, we're here in the flesh," Hector said, throwing his arms wide. "Ready to make merry with you and yours."

Lord Clement glanced toward Meg and seemed to freeze in place for a moment. He quickly recovered and smiled at her. "And who is this beauty you have brought with you? I must have an introduction immediately."

"Surely you don't need to be introduced to my sister after all these years?" Hector teased with a hearty laugh that made Meg cringe.

She lifted her chin and looked Lord Clement in the eye, eager to get the greeting over and done with. "My lord."

Lord Clement's lips parted in obvious surprise. "Lady Margaret?"

"Meg," she said, nodding to him. "No one has called me by my full name since our mother passed."

Lord Clement shook his head suddenly. "Forgive me, but I would never have recognized you."

"I thought the same of you," she murmured, and then fidgeted under his startlingly direct gaze. The handsome devil had surprised her with his improved appearance but he was still a man to be wary of. He had kept her brother away from home for so much of the last few years.

Lord Clement drew closer, his smile growing wider as he came. "It is a surprise to see you but a happy one. Welcome to The Vynes, my lady."

She was about to dip into a curtsy but he reached for her hand instead. She placed her gloved hand in his larger one and looked up into the darkest, bluest eyes she'd ever seen and trembled. They reminded her of the sea, of her home shores, and she gulped in shock as he bowed over her hand in a courtly fashion. "Thank you, my lord."

He released her hand slowly, a look of puzzlement creeping into his expression as he drew back. His eyes narrowed on her face. "I say, are you warm enough?"

Meg was becoming entirely too warm with all the attention in the room fixed on her. She had kept her coat on despite being indoors but Lord Clement was having a heating affect on all parts of her body. "I believe so."

"Good. Good," he said, quickly glancing at Hector.

"About time too," Hector promised, slapping Lord Clement on the shoulder and drawing him back from Meg. "She kept promising me she'd turn into an icicle at every stop on the way here."

"I hardly blame her." Lord Clement frowned, glancing at Meg then away again. "It has been colder than usual for this time of year. I would not have subjected my sisters to such a journey."

Meg felt vindicated by Lord Clement's remark and glared at her brother. "I warned you it was entirely too cold for such a trip. The poor grooms must be frozen solid."

Lord Clement winced. "Your brother barely notices the weather. I'll make enquiries about your servants and make sure they are amply warmed."

"I would appreciate that."

Lord Clement stepped back farther and Hector began to regale him with the details of their journey, including the *charming* inns they'd stayed in along the way. Those inns had not been charming but frighteningly drafty in her opinion. She dreaded spending another night in them for the return journey home.

Meg inched closer to the countess' side but she felt Lord Clement's attention return to regard her. "Mother, why did you not tell me to expect my friends for Christmas?"

"I wanted to surprise you," she teased him. "Call it my Christmas wish for you to be with your friends again."

He shook his head and glanced at Meg. "I hate that I was the last to know."

"Not by much. Coming here was a surprise to me too," Meg said quickly. "I only learned what Hector planned the day before we left home."

"How very like him to leave everything until the last moment." Lord Clement shook his head. "Rest assured nothing has been left to chance in London. The new townhouse in Half-Moon Street will be ready to welcome you in the New Year."

Meg frowned at Lord Clement and then her brother. "What new townhouse?"

"Good grief, now you've gone and spoiled the surprise entirely," Hector complained to his friend.

Meg gulped. Surely he couldn't mean to leave her in Dorset to manage the estate alone. "Hector, what is going on?"

Lord Clement winced. "I am sorry. I thought you would have told her."

"I'll explain later," Hector warned Meg.

What had Hector done? "Why do you need a London townhouse?"

"Because we will be living in there soon. I cannot have a woman at my bachelor apartment on Clarges Street, even if she is a relation. Makes sense to establish a permanent residence before the season starts," he announced as he turned away. "How's that new horse of yours coming along, Clement?"

Meg gaped and then cast a quick glance at the countess. She tried to smile. London and the season, parties and pretty gowns and stumbling through reels and waltzes as if one were happy, was unthinkable right now. She was still in mourning, even if Hector believed otherwise.

Hector *had* broached the subject of finding a husband on the long journey from the coast but she had refused to consider it. Was he giving her no choice?

"Fine. Fine." Lord Clement glanced over his shoulder at Meg, frowning. "Don't look so worried. It is a lovely little spot. Very close to everything."

"Yes indeed," Hector promised. "She'll enjoy shopping and the parties very much."

"But Hector—"

"Later, Meg." Hector drew Lord Clement firmly away from her.

Meg's heart began to race with renewed anxiety. What else hadn't Hector told her about lately? This trip, and now a home in London. A season she hadn't asked for.

When Lord Clement glanced her way one more time, Meg studied her fingers. An uneasy sensation was growing in her stomach. She was supposed to do as her brother decided, the way she would have obeyed their father. The temptation to run away was very strong right now. If only she were a little older, she could make her own decisions.

Lady Vyne drew closer. "Have you done any preparation for the coming season?"

"No," she said in a tiny voice. She glanced at her brother, but he wouldn't meet her eye anymore. Panic began to overload her senses.

"Well, no matter. There's still plenty of time." The countess smiled warmly. "I think you might be warm enough now to venture upstairs to your bedchamber. I've had everything prepared for days. Come, let's get you settled. Do excuse us, gentlemen."

Hector nodded but Lord Clement murmured her name softly as she passed him by.

Once beyond the room, Meg's despair only grew worse as she shivered anew in the chill air of the hall. Hector should have confided in her.

"I wish I could be in London to support you finding a husband," Lady Vyne whispered. "Unfortunately, my husband is in poor health and I cannot leave."

Dread filled Meg at the news. "I am very sorry to hear that."

Having the countess by her side might have made the situation bearable.

"Not to worry. Your brother wrote of his

intentions to bring you out when he accepted my invitation to come for the holiday, and I will be very happy, very honored, to offer any assistance I can to prepare you while you are with us."

"You're very kind," she said at last.

"Nonsense. It's the least I can do for my friend's daughter now that she has gone. I look forward to meeting your future husband one day, too."

Meg nodded miserably and started up the next flight of stairs at the countess' urging.

There was no reason to confess to the countess that the thought of a London season terrified her. Meg had hoped to marry one day, but not now. She felt the insult of her brother's rush very keenly.

She had seen the signs of Hector's restlessness and shrugged them off. How could she have been so blind to the truth—his unhappiness was with Meg's unmarried state!

The countess suddenly clucked her tongue. "Now who do we have here? Are you not supposed to be taking your lessons?"

Meg looked up in surprise. Three children, two pretty girls and a tiny boy, were looking down on them, their serious little faces pressed between the railings. The girls rushed down to greet their mother and Meg, dragging the small boy with them. "We waited ever so long."

The countess smiled and gestured to Meg. "My dears, this is our good friend, Lady Margaret Stockwick. You must make Meg feel welcome."

The girls, Esther and Molly, curtsied and the little boy, Evan, made a bow when urged.

Meg couldn't help but smile at them all. They were adorable and reminded Meg of Lord Clement at that age. There had been another girl too, one closer to Meg's age, but she had been married off some time ago. "You are both so pretty," she murmured to the girls, and then looked at the boy. "And you, sir, are very handsome, too."

The children giggled, apparently delighted by her compliments. One of the girls took her hand and drew her along, surrounded by the Vyne family. She was taken into a bright room and then the children fled soundlessly.

Meg glanced around a bedchamber fit for royalty and stood gaping.

"I think this room will do very nicely for you. What do you think, my dear?"

This bedchamber exceeded her every expectation for comfort.

The walls were papered in yellow striped silk and a thick cornflower-blue silk comforter covered the bed. The room was warm and light and so much nicer than the one she'd left behind; nicer than any room she'd ever stayed in before for that matter. There was a fire already burning in the grate.

"It's lovely," she promised.

The maids had already begun unpacking Meg's trunks, storing her belongings in the tall oak chests that lined the walls. Meg collected a few of her more personal items and set them on the mirrored table between the tall sash windows. She glanced outside, noticing thick vines, though dormant now, bracketed her window.

She turned around to ask what flowers the vine would produce—until she noticed the maids were unpacking gowns she'd never seen before. She saw bright colors instead of the somber grays and lavender gowns she'd asked to be packed for this short holiday. Her familiar clothing was nowhere to be seen.

The countess asked a servant to add more fuel to the fire and then bid them all to go. She came to stand beside Meg. "Hector didn't mention moving to London, did he?"

"No."

"And you'd not intended to rejoin society yet."

She lifted her chin, determined not to fall to pieces in front of the countess. "I didn't."

"I am so sorry. All of this must be quite a shock. I know what it's like to have no voice, no say in any decision."

That was an understatement if ever she'd heard of one. "Three days ago, I had a home," Meg whispered.

"You will become accustomed to the change of pace in due time."

"Yes, I am sure one can grow accustomed to being treated as cattle, too." She swallowed the lump of horror that had lodged in her throat. "I think my brother will foist me off onto the first man who notices me."

"It won't be as bad as all that," the countess promised. "You'll make friends easily."

"What of the friends I have already?" She fought back tears. "He didn't even let me say goodbye to anyone."

The countess settled an arm around Meg's shoulders and drew her close. "He should have told you about the decision he made when your father died. What can we do? We women hardly ever have a say in our lives."

Meg allowed her tears to slide down her cheeks unchecked then. Hector had been planning to be rid of her for months and months and never told her. But he had certainly told the countess, and Lord Clement must know, too. They were best friends. Meg was nothing but a burden.

The countess rubbed Meg's arm briskly, trying to bolster her spirits. "It will be all right, I swear. I will do my best to help you. I will write to my friends and discover who will be in London when you are. They will help you if I ask."

It was a kind offer, but Meg didn't feel reassured. She had never felt so powerless before. She moved to the window and stared blindly at the view.

The Vynes was set in the center of the bowl-shaped valley, and she could see a small slice of it from this room's window. Everything was white and uninviting. "Has it been a harsh winter so far?"

"It has. I'm hoping the weather clears soon because it becomes quite dreadful when the children are shut up inside for excessive time."

"Yes, children do love their freedom," Meg agreed, wrapping her arms around her chest. She had lost hers when her father had died.

Chapter Four

Otis invaded his mother's bedchamber the next morning without knocking too loudly and risking waking his father in the next room. Mother customarily rose early while Father slept late. And he had a sour temper if anyone dared wake him earlier than elevenses.

Morning was the perfect time to see Mother. She'd been impossible to catch alone since the Stockwick siblings had arrived yesterday afternoon.

He glanced at the connecting door as he crossed the room just to be sure they were really alone. He kissed her cheek and sat beside her at the window overlooking the white gardens around the manor house. "It is going to be a beautiful day," he promised.

"I'm glad," she murmured. "The children

could do with some fresh air."

"Not Evan," Otis warned. "His nurse said his nose was running like a brook all night."

Mother nodded. "Just us girls then."

Mother was already dressed for the outing, donning her warmest wool coat to keep away the chill. "Mother, what are Hector and Margaret Stockwick doing here," he demanded.

"Well, we couldn't very well invite Meg to stay without inviting Hector, too. I just couldn't bear to think of her alone in that huge house for one more Christmas."

"They do have servants."

Mother rubbed her hands together and blew on them. "You must guess how hard this year will be for her. Family must stick together."

"Yes, I'm aware of their growing estrangement, but the timing is troubling. Anyone can see just looking at her that she'd rather be anywhere else."

Mother sighed. "She's been in mourning since her mother died, and perhaps before that, too. Justine was ill for so long. It's too long for a girl her age to be sequestered away from society with just servants for company."

"She has a brother," Otis reminded her.

"But he's never there. You know he's not."

Otis sighed and glanced outside. "It's not my fault he prefers London. I have tried…"

"Her letters have torn at my heart and my

conscience for too long." Mother settled her hand over his. "I don't blame you. I know you've done all you could to make him leave London and take care of his responsibilities at home, but it seems he will not do it."

"He's a stubborn bastard," Otis admitted. "The estate must be falling to wrack and ruin without a firm hand at the reins."

"Meg does what she can to keep the estate profitable."

"At least that is something." If only things were different. The Stockwicks' estate in Dorset had once thrived under the late Lord Stockwick, or it had before the mother had died.

"Be that as it may, I'm convinced Meg just needs a little reassurance that it is all right to set her mourning aside and think of the future. In a way, she will always be in mourning for the parents she loves and misses. But she has to face a life without them eventually. You'll hardly notice her. I promise."

That wasn't likely. The changes in Margaret Stockwick had knocked the wind out of his sails momentarily. She had not spoken very much at all yesterday, but she had once been bold and outspoken. Traits that had set her apart from other girls he'd known. As a child, she'd been intrepid, always following them around when he'd visited the Stockwicks' estate by the sea.

Otis raked a hand through his hair again. Margaret was miserable. He'd seen that very clearly. She was not as she once was, and that was a tragedy. "She has no idea how her brother intends to spend the next years, does she?"

"None at all, I'm afraid. We had a little chat when she was settling into her room last night. It's come as something of a shock that Hector is bringing her out of mourning early. I really thought he would tell her about moving to London before now, too."

Otis had seen Margaret's shock with his own eyes too at the mention of London. The poor girl—woman, he corrected himself—was practically reeling at the idea of entering the marriage mart. It had to be done, of course, it was the right thing to do, but obviously done the wrong way in Margaret's case. "I'll have a word with him."

"Not every gentleman worries about the happiness of women as you do," she said, in praise of him. "Would that your friend were the same. Meg has been so sad for such a long time. Losing both her parents in such a way has been very painful for her. You know how close she was to them. Hector's decision to force her into society like this is not the way."

Otis caught his mother's eye. "So you and

Hector are conspiring against Margaret now. How long has this been going on?"

"It wasn't like that. I asked your father if she could come, expecting a refusal, and he had no objection for a change. I thought a short time away from home would do her the world of good, but I did not know then that Hector intended to sell the estate. What can be done to stop him if he does not like the place? Nothing, unfortunately."

"The estate has great potential. Selling now would be a mistake I intend to talk Hector out of," Otis decided. "It could be a very good situation if Hector would just apply himself."

Mother sighed. "Hector has no interest in managing a country estate, and you know it. He's happier gadding about in London with you and your friends."

"Well, those days are behind me. My life is here now with you and the children."

"I'm glad to see you here but you know you don't have to stay for us." Mother looked up at him and smiled quickly. "I'd like your promise that you will make Meg feel at home here during her stay."

Otis regarded his mother warily. "And how do you expect me to do that?"

"You could talk to her about the delights of London. She's lived a sheltered life by the sea, and everything will seem very strange and overwhelming at first."

"She is my best friend's sister. Men who pay too much attention to their best friend's sisters create discord and suspicion."

Mother regarded him with amusement. "Do you fear she will fall in love with you?"

"Don't be absurd. I would never allow that to happen."

"Love is always beyond our control, my son" she warned him, and then burst into a grin. "What would you do if she did set her sights on marrying you instead of preparing for a London season? Once upon a time, her mother and I thought something might happen between you."

"Something?" he asked, although he knew what Mother was about to say. She hoped for grandchildren as much as Father did. But she wanted him to wed happily, and with more love than she'd ever known in her marriage. And Mother was exceedingly fond of Margaret. It was not surprising she wished for a match between them.

Her brow arched. "Do you not think Meg is pretty?"

"That is a foolish question. Of course Margaret is a very pretty girl."

Mother smiled in delight at his answer. "Bright, too."

Not so clever as to realize her brother was

keen to marry her off. "It is an unfortunate failing of yours to always wish for the impossible," he warned his mother.

"I wish for happiness, my son. For all of us. Especially Meg."

"Mother, you are a hopeless romantic but you are bound to be disappointed in me," he warned. Otis glanced at his mother quickly and forced a smile. "I have something to tell you?"

"You've made another foolish wager with your father."

Otis gaped. "How did you hear?"

"Your father gloated about it when he came to see me last night. I assume you know what you're doing?"

"I do have something of a plan, but only three months to marry someone good." Otis grasped his mother's hand quickly. "I'm sorry I did not consult with you first. I hope Father did not upset you."

"He tried," she said softly and wouldn't meet his eyes.

His parents' marriage had forever been volatile. "Mother, did he mention that the wager could have consequences for all of us? For you and the children too?"

"Yes, that part particularly pleased him." She sat back with a sigh. "He gloated that he'd backed you into a corner. He thinks to have his way."

"I am going to marry, Mother, but not the woman he's chosen for me." Otis' stomach clenched with worry though. "And I promised to look after you and the children. I will find a suitable bride and I will win your freedom in the end too."

She shook her head. "All I want is for you to be happy."

"Winning the wager will make me very happy."

Mother glanced toward the connecting door. "Once upon a time, I would have stayed with him out of affection."

Otis rubbed a hand over his face. "What can I do to make you smile?"

"Marry for love in your own time and move away," she replied. "What is done is done and the past cannot be changed. I have to live with the consequences of my decision to marry such a vindictive creature. Promise you will never become like him."

"I won't." Otis heard voices coming from his father's room. It must be nearing elevenses. "I have to go."

"Yes, your friends will be wondering where you are." Mother tilted her cheek up and Otis quickly pressed a kiss to her cool skin.

"Hector doesn't rise before noon."

She smiled quickly. "Meg rises early, and she should be your friend, too. She will need you in the coming months. Help her where I cannot."

Otis sighed. He couldn't refuse his mother this one boon. He would be in London looking for a wife at the same time Meg was there too. "I'll do my best."

"You'll find her in the library at this hour, I expect." She stood and brushed her gown straight. "Now I had better go to the children before they come looking for me and earn a punishment from him."

Otis thought that an excellent idea. Father did not like to see his children anywhere but in the gardens or the nursery floor above. He bid his mother goodbye and turned in the direction of the library.

Chapter Five

The Vyne estate in Derbyshire was a bleak place in the middle of winter.

Meg huddled at one end of a large window seat in the vast library, under a thick wool blanket to keep the cold at bay. She stared out at the nonexistent view with a heavy heart. There was nothing to see but fog and snow-covered ground outside her window. At times it seemed like there were no clear skies on the horizon. She was surrounded by the weather and by a family that she didn't belong to.

Hector had abandoned her company almost as soon as they had arrived. He had disappeared with Lord Clement last night after dinner without saying when he'd return or when she might talk to him about London. She'd heard he'd ridden out early that day, despite the terrible weather.

She gritted her teeth. Her future had been decided for her. She would move to London, marry, and that was that. It hurt that Hector had run away from the conversation he'd promised her.

She pulled the blankets higher and settled deeper into the pillows behind her back. She had chosen a spot that afforded her a good view of the front drive and the stables. She might know the moment Hector returned. Until he did, there was nothing for her to do but wait.

The door creaked open slowly, and Meg froze as a presence entered the room slowly.

"Am I disturbing you?" Lord Clement asked softly.

Meg twisted around, grievously disappointed to see her brother was not standing there, too. "No. I was just about to leave."

Lord Clement quickly held up his hands. "No. No. Don't move from that lovely warm spot. I didn't intend to drive you from the room. I actually wanted to talk to you."

Meg regarded him warily. "What do you want from me?"

"Nothing," he said with a quick smile. He hovered by the door, but searched the room with his eyes. He put his hands behind his back and kept a distance. "I wanted to see if there was anything you might need."

"There is nothing I need," she promised, hoping he would go about his business soon and depart. "I have my book and your mother will send for me soon, I'm sure."

He looked around again. "Where is your maid?"

"I've never had one."

He shook his head and muttered something under his breath. "I'll have our Gladys assigned to you for your stay. She was with my other sister when she had her season. You'll find her invaluable."

"I don't need anything from you," she insisted, and then scowled at him. "Shouldn't you be with my brother?"

"He's up?" Lord Clement drew closer. "I assumed he would still be abed at this hour."

"He went out. I assumed he was with you."

"Not with me. I have responsibilities here that cannot be shirked even for visitors." He sighed. "But I am free now."

Meg was quite tired of lies, half-truths, and omissions. Lord Clement was a rogue, cut from the same cloth as her brother. "There's no need to pretend interest in me when you must long to be elsewhere. Hector has made it clear gentlemen have better things to do than sit about the countryside sipping tea."

"I'm not sure why your brother would

include me in that statement, but I spend a great deal of time in the country sipping tea and enjoy it too. Actually, I only spend about six weeks in London each year, seeing the solicitor who manages my affairs and attending a few parties I cannot get out of. The rest of the year, I'm here. But I was forced to spend months away from the estate once. Hated every moment of it."

Meg studied Lord Clement, and then wet her lips. His statement seemed honest enough, but that would mean her brother had been lying to her. "Hector led me to believe he was with you in London for most of last year."

Lord Clement appeared surprised by that. "I was with him for only a few weeks and Hector can attest to my impatience to return home I'm sure."

She stared at him in astonishment. "Do you really prefer the country?"

"Indeed I do," he said and then winced. "Hector does not, however. Your brother has not accepted an invitation to visit The Vynes in an age. I am astonished that he came this year for the holiday."

"I see," Meg's eyes pricked with tears. If Hector hadn't been with Lord Clement in London then what had he been doing with his life? Obviously whatever it was, he didn't want her to know about it. Meg was stunned.

Meg looked away and brought her fingers to her lips. "Hector's comments have led me to believe you a bad influence on him. I blamed you for taking my brother away when I needed him most."

Lord Clement crossed the room to stand a few feet away. "If he'd spoken the truth, I must have seemed a heartless beast to you. I am sorry you were misinformed."

Meg frowned at the comment. "It is Hector who should apologize. Wherever he may be?"

"I can have him found and brought back if you like. We have enough servants to wrestle him out of any tavern." Lord Clement leaned her way to whisper. "It wouldn't be the first time, honestly."

"That will not be necessary," she said sadly. Her brother should want to be with her, and Hector would only resent her even more than he must already were he dragged back to The Vynes.

Lord Clement moved again, stopping at her side. She looked up into his eyes, so blue and kind as they held her gaze, and her heart fluttered for no good reason. He smiled slowly. "Are you sure there is nothing I can do for you? Another blanket or pillow, or a discussion of the best shops to patronize in London. Mother suggested I might help you prepare for your season."

"I assure you, I do not want to think about London right now but thank you for your kindness."

"Well, then. Another time perhaps. Have you been outside today?" Meg shook her head and Lord Clement's eyes lit up. "Mother is planning an outing with my sisters soon."

Meg dropped her gaze. "It is snowing," she noted. "And cold."

Lord Clement suddenly sat down beside her. "I adore this time of year here. When you are out amongst the snow as it falls, it is as if you are the only person in the world."

"That sounds lonely."

"Believe me, it's not when your sisters have been squabbling all morning." He pressed two fingers to his brow. "The noise can be quite overpowering."

"That would make a difference, I suppose," she conceded. "But I wouldn't know what that's like to fight with my sibling. Hector and I don't disagree very often."

She and Hector were as quiet as church mice, usually. And if they had a disagreement, she realized, as they did now, Hector tended to make himself scarce.

"You could join us for a short walk out," Lord Clement pressed. "I remember you were quite energetic when we were younger. And with such views as to be had in Dorset, I'd be surprised if you had grown tired of wandering the cliffs." He caught her eye, his expression hopeful.

She did not think he would recall anything of her nature after all this time. It had been years since he'd visited her home. She sighed. "Out to where?"

"Anywhere will do. Everything seems different when the world is covered in snow," he promised. "Even the pig pens can seem magical."

Meg laughed at that. "Except for the smell."

But a walk outside with others sounded like a pleasant way to pass the time given the way Lord Clement described it. Perhaps if she wasn't alone out there, she would not feel more lonely than she already was. But if she went out, she feared she could miss Hector's return. There were things they needed to talk about. "Perhaps tomorrow."

"Excellent. I will let my mother and sisters know that you might join us for the morning walk."

Meg nodded slowly.

"Is that a good book?" Lord Clement asked suddenly, gesturing to her lap. The blanket must have lowered upon his arrival to reveal the book she had placed there.

She glanced at it, and sighed. "It is quite terrible."

Lord Clement's face crinkled with confusion. "If it's dreadful, why are you holding it still? Do you want another?"

She revealed the book to him and spread her hands over the leather binding. "This was the last book my father and I were reading together. We made a pact to never not finish a book, even if it was terrible."

A look of understanding crossed his face. "I see, and you've been reading it all this time?"

"I try to. I just can't seem to finish," she confessed.

"May I?" he asked, holding out one hand.

Meg placed the book in his hand and watched the viscount skim through the early pages. He easily found her place midway through the book and turned it towards the light from the window.

Lord Clement began to read to her, his voice ringing out strongly in the quiet of the library.

And she was transported into the world that her father and her had once inhabited together. It really was a dreadful book, but fascinating all the same.

Lord Clement continued to read, turning two more pages before he finally looked up. "How far along did your father read before you took your turn?" he asked.

"We each took a chapter," she confessed,

hoping he would not mind.

Lord Clement returned to the story, and Meg could not stop watching his expressive face.

She had not expected such kindness from him or his interest in her. He was unexpected. He was the last person Meg ever thought would do something just to make her happy. Her father had been like that. Always ready with a smile. Forever willing to lift her up when she was cast down.

It was hard to believe that the man sitting across from her was the same one she had dreaded spending Christmas with.

Meg felt peace wash over her at last and, for a moment, she stopped grieving for what was gone. But then she remembered so quick and so painfully that her eyes filled with tears. She looked away, and Lord Clement's voice died away slowly.

"I say, Margaret, are you all right?"

She nodded but she could not stop the tears that began to flow down her cheeks. She wiped them away quickly, but Lord Clement suddenly pressed his handkerchief into her hands.

"Here, use this instead," he whispered. "Can't have your fingers getting frostbite now, can we?"

"It's not quite that cold," she told him, and he laughed, his rich, deep voice filling the room with happiness. And she was cured of her melancholy for the moment. She found the strength to laugh along with him, too. Meg dabbed at her cheeks, and then she turned to face him. "Thank you," she whispered.

"You're very welcome," he promised.

His eyes were still kind, and she saw in him at last the young boy she had once known. She had called the boy by his given name—Otis. She did not remember when exactly she had stopped. But the pair were not so different. Both had made her laugh. She glanced at the handkerchief she was twisting in her hands, the one she'd been crying her tears over.

"Please keep it," Otis whispered. "You might need to use it to block your ears when my voice becomes intolerably hoarse."

He smiled as he turned the page to a new chapter and crossed his long legs and began to read again.

She leaned toward him and placed her hand on his arm. "You don't have to continue reading. You've done enough," she suggested.

"I need to find out what happens at the end of the story now," he told her, covering her hand with his. "I've already missed half the book. To stop now when there is more to go would be intolerable. I always like to know how a story ends."

Assured he meant it, Meg let him keep the

book and sat back, resting her head against the wall behind her. Otis told a wonderful story, and she was soon enthralled in that world once more, but this time with none of the sadness she had experienced since her father's passing.

She could not account for how different she felt with Otis sitting beside her. Meg clutched the blanket closer around her body and lay her cheek upon her knees and was soon swept away by the soothing quality of his voice. There were so few men with such patience for storytelling. Hector had none. She appreciated Otis for his generous spirit more than words could say.

"My siblings routinely fall asleep when I read to them," Otis murmured with a quick glance in her direction. "I hope you're not in danger of doing the same."

"I'm not sleepy," she replied quickly, lest he stop altogether.

"Are you sure?" he asked in a teasing tone.

"I was just resting my eyes," she promised as she sat up straight. "See. Wide awake."

Determined not to succumb to the lull of his voice, she took the book from him, found the last words he'd spoken, and commenced to read aloud to him.

Otis inched closer, watching the page as she finished the chapter.

Continuing the story had felt better, too. Easier. She was not assailed by memories of

Father reading to her that last final time he'd had the strength for it. Now she could remember Otis' voice and the comfort his kindness had brought her.

Otis sighed heavily. "Is that better?"

Meg nodded quickly and placed a scrap of paper inside the book to mark the place she had stopped and set it aside. "I can't thank you enough," she whispered. "I think I can continue on my own now."

Otis smiled widely, and captured her hands. His grip was firm, reassuring. "Oh, don't say you won't have my company again. I really must know what happens next. Perhaps after our walk with my siblings tomorrow, we can continue to read the next chapter. I'm quite eager to discover what happens next."

He sounded so sincere, Meg smiled. "Me too."

"It really is quite a dreadful book," he said suddenly. "I cannot thank you enough for allowing me the privilege of reading it with you."

Meg giggled, turning her hand over in Otis' grip. "You're welcome. I never really thought you had an interest in books. Hector has no patience to visit our small library."

"Oh, I am interested in quite a number of things. I dare say you will be pleasantly surprised once we become reacquainted properly," he promised. He leaned forward and pressed his lips to her temple suddenly. "It's good to see you smiling at last."

Meg shivered as he drew back. She met his gaze and saw shock in his. He was sitting so close that her breath faltered.

Otis cleared his throat. "I don't know why I did that."

"It meant nothing, I know," she assured him, looking down at their joined hands. He had kissed her as if she was one of his sisters. The women of his family were so lucky to have a warm man like this in their lives. But the last thing Meg wanted was awkwardness between them.

She lifted her gaze slowly. Otis was watching her face with a half smile playing over his lips. His grip on her fingers eased and then his fingers stroked over her palm. Meg's heart began to beat a little faster. She should push him away, but she couldn't seem to do what was expected of her. She wet her lips. "You should go," she suggested to him. "Before someone sees us together and misunderstands."

"I suppose I should."

Yet, Otis did not get up to leave. His fingers toyed with hers, gently stroking them until her face grew quite warm. "What are you doing," Meg asked softly. Otis confused her.

"I have no idea," he confessed. "You are my

best friend's younger sister," he said finally as his light touch slid upward to her wrist, and then her arm. "Do you know I am not supposed to think of my friend's sister's as women, or," he smiled slowly as his eyes drifted over her features and down across her body before he looked up, "or to find them as attractive as I do you."

Meg's blush grew hotter until she was sure she couldn't blush any harder.

There was a strange tension between them now—and then Otis suddenly darted towards her and pressed his lips to hers. His kiss was sweet, soft, and oh so gentle. His fingertips lingered on her cheek, warm but gentle as he cupped her skull. A lingering pleasure that curled her toes in her slippers and made her senses soar to incredible heights. She leaned into the kiss, delighting in the forbidden thrill of attraction and desire, hoping it would never end.

She had been kissed before, but she did not remember enjoying those as much as she did Otis'. She was sorry when he drew back with a heavy sigh.

Meg frowned at him. "Why did you kiss me that time?"

Otis shook his head. "I don't know. I swear it will not happen again." He frowned so hard that deep lines appeared on his brow. "Um, excuse me. I had better go arrange for you to have that maid I promised. It's probably best you not be alone with me again."

"You might be right, my lord." Meg nodded, still a bit stunned by his kisses and how she felt about them. She was not offended or even upset with him. She wouldn't mind another too but Lord Clement quickly got to his feet and moved away.

He walked toward the door, but looked back over his shoulder a few times before he got there.

Meg noticed that he seemed unsettled by his actions. It made her like him even more. She would never have believed a rogue or a scoundrel would be ill at ease after kissing anyone. Perhaps he wasn't so bad after all.

He finally slipped from the room with one last lingering glance in her direction. Meg wrapped her arms about the book and laughed softly as she looked outside. A shaft of sunlight had fought through the clouds above The Vynes at last, and the estate was instantly warmer than it had once seemed.

Chapter Six

If he just pretended everything was normal, he would survive his latest indiscretion unscathed. That is what Otis told himself from the moment he woke the next morning until he faced Lady Margaret over breakfast. And when he saw her smile his way, Otis imagined any number of completely inappropriate thoughts revolving around kissing his friend's sister again.

Before his completely unprovoked kiss, he could have gone weeks and months without giving Lady Margaret Stockwick a second or even first thought. Before he'd kissed Margaret, he'd never imagined his best friend's sister might be worth risking a friendship over just so he could have the pleasure of kissing her again.

But as the breakfast progressed, and her eyes

sought his time and again, he considered renewing his acquaintance with her a most intriguing opportunity. It had certainly been a while since he'd done anything without thinking the matter through properly. Considering the consequences and the needs of the family first had become second nature up until yesterday.

"I think I've had enough, thank you," Otis decided and allowed a servant to remove his breakfast plate. He sat back, noting Margaret requested more tea but ate little.

She looked so pretty that morning, dressed all in green velvet. She looked as if she had rested well last night, too, and she was smiling whenever Hector spoke to her.

Otis wished he could say he'd passed as good a night. He had been keenly aware that her bedchamber was not so very far away from his, and that he found her terribly attractive. He buried his nose in his teacup again, and scolded himself roundly. He would not kiss Margaret again—not without her permission or invitation.

Hector gobbled up one last slice of ham and glanced his way. "A word, Clement."

Otis nodded, wondering if Hector had already seen that he was paying attention to Margaret and meant to warn him off.

He drained the dregs of his tea, casting a

casual eye over the waiting table as he rose. Mother seemed happy, but she always was when Father absented himself from dining with them. His siblings were content for the moment and not squabbling. His eyes were drawn back to Margaret but her expression filled him with unease. Would she have told Hector what he'd done with her lips yesterday?

Hector threw aside his napkin and strode out.

Fearing the worst, Otis joined him in the hall. "Where were you last night?"

"Renewing my acquaintance with George Moore," Hector said with a sly smile.

"And his sister too, I suppose," Otis murmured quietly. "She's trouble."

"After the year I've had, I enjoy that sort of trouble." Hector scowled. "For heaven's sake, don't go all *Meg* on me."

"What does that mean?"

"One mustn't have any fun. One must mourn forever," Hector said with an exaggerated feminine tone that might have been a poor attempt to imitate his sister.

Otis checked that the hall was still empty. He had no experience with losing a member of his family but he hoped he displayed more compassion to his loved ones than Hector seemed to. "Just a friendly warning."

"Anyone would think our father was a

saint," Hector grumbled, rubbing the back of his neck. "He had a woman the year Mother fell ill."

Otis was surprised to hear it. Lady Stockwick had been very ill for a long time but he had thought the couple had been closer than ever. Margaret seemed to idolize her late father. She would be shattered to know he had not been faithful. "I assume your sister has no idea?"

"None. She'd never believe me."

Thank heavens for small mercies. "Telling her now would be cruel. Women tend to become emotional upon hearing about betrayals of that nature."

"And knowing my luck, it would turn her forever away from the idea of marriage. I'll never be rid of her if she found out." Hector smiled suddenly. "I was wondering if I might borrow a few pounds from you."

"What do you need money for?"

"George Moore."

"Why couldn't you leave it alone?" Otis murmured quietly. Hector gambled too often and recklessly for his taste. It was one of the reasons he was happy not to be in London with him very often.

"I have to try to win my money back." Hector nodded. "The bastard cheated me out of my money."

"If you didn't gamble while drinking it wouldn't be so easy." George Moore had a temper when there were winnings owed to him. Otis dug in his pocket to see what change he carried, hoping it would be enough. A few notes and a handful of coins was all he had right now. He held them out and Hector took all of it with a grin.

"I'll pay you back of course but I really must be on my way."

"So soon?"

"Meg seems to be settled in now with your mother and really doesn't need me," Hector announced.

"Of course Margaret needs you," Otis insisted, remembering yesterday's conversation. "You are her brother. The most important man in her life right now."

"She needs the company of other women. She also needs to prepare for her season and marriage. I cannot help with that. Lady Vyne has consented to take Mother's role in educating her on such matters. So I am going to absent myself until Christmas Day. After Twelfth Night, we'll head for London and I'll start introducing her around Town. With the dowry I'm prepared to bestow, I'm sure she will attract sufficient interest to find herself a husband."

Otis recoiled from Hector a little. There

were days Otis did not understand Hector at all. He would never treat one of his sisters with so little consideration.

But Hector was right about the interest Margaret could stir up in London. She was pretty and bright and dowered, but she was not looking forward to the season the way many women did. He wished Mother could be in London with her then. She would keep any scoundrels away from her and steer her toward a good man.

If Otis found himself in London at that time, he could introduce her to any good men he knew.

After the emotional few years she'd experienced, she might need good friends as she made the most important decision of her life. Otis studied Hector warily. She clearly couldn't count on her brother to be patient. Otis was almost afraid Hector might just approve the first man who asked for her hand to be rid of her.

If Hector learned they had kissed, he might insist *Otis* marry Margaret, whether she wished to or not.

Although…if Otis did offer for Margaret, and was accepted, he would win the bet with his father with time to spare.

Otis turned at the sound of raised voices. His mother and sisters were finally leaving the morning room, while the boy was being dragged back upstairs by his nurse. Margaret was bringing up the rear.

Otis glanced around but found only empty air where Hector had stood.

"For heaven's sake," he cursed under his breath, and then smiled as the ladies joined him. He clapped his hands together once and rubbed them briskly. "So are we all ready to brave the outdoors at last?"

He looked at each of them. His sisters and mother exclaimed that they were. Margaret was quieter in her response, but she too agreed she was ready to face the outdoors. He was glad she could be coaxed outside with them at last.

"Well, then hurry up and get your coats," he told them all, moving as if he was about to rush outside without them. His siblings were usually quick, so they rushed for the waiting servants and began to rug up.

Margaret was first dressed and slid past him in the narrow hall without meeting his gaze. The sweet scent of honeysuckle left in her wake was utterly intoxicating. He'd found the scent on her skin most distracting yesterday, too.

Otis allowed everyone to file from the house ahead of him.

Mother was slowest, which ensured she and Otis brought up the rear together. Meg was swept away by the girls up the garden path, and that was for the best. He needed to talk to Mother without being overheard. "Stockwick intends to leave Margaret entirely to your care. He's slipped away again and won't be back until Christmas Day."

"Good."

He looked at his mother in surprise. "Good?"

Mother huffed. "She spent the whole of last night and this morning waiting to talk to him. If I can convince her he'll be gone for a few days, she might consent to having a little fun, or considering the future. Perhaps you can help with that."

He glanced at her with suspicion. "What did you have in mind?"

"Be attentive. Boost her confidence. Every woman wants to be admired by a gentleman of taste."

"I'm sure she knows her value."

"I'm not so sure anymore," Mother warned. "Did you know Meg once had a suitor?"

"Hector never mentioned that."

"Local lad. Hector introduced them. The fellow had ambitions that included leaving England. Meg was devastated when it was proved he was only interested in her for her dowry and planned to leave her behind as soon as their vows were spoken."

Knowing Margaret had been disappointed

in love before did explain why she might be reluctant to venture onto the marriage mart. He would be, too, under those circumstances. "Is that why she never married, because her heart was broken?"

"That and losing the parents she adored to illness and grief. She hasn't had a chance to impress anyone since. Let's hope her next suitor has more staying power and a truer heart," Mother whispered and then strode forward.

Ahead, his sisters were whispering while Margaret walked alone. He had noticed the girls and Meg seemed to get along well this visit, almost as well as Margaret and Mother did. Margaret's devotion to her family was one quality they had in common.

He hurried to catch up to her.

Margaret seemed surprised when he fell into step with her. "Are you enjoying the walk?" he asked as she stopped and looked around for the rest of the group.

"Yes," she promised with a sigh. "This is just what I need. Peace and quiet."

"Yes, peace and…" Otis spun around quickly. Walks with his sisters were never quiet. And he could not see either one of them. Mother had fallen behind, nudging snow off a statue with the tip of her finger. All there was to see was snow-covered shrubbery.

His tension increased. It would be a surprise

attack at any moment then.

Otis rushed toward Margaret, arms spread. "No, not today!" he cried out.

But it was too late. Balls of snow pelted down upon them in a thick white shower.

Margaret screamed in fright.

Thinking to protect her, Otis put his arms around her head and shoulders. "I'll punish them for this," he assured Margaret.

Margaret fell to the ground, and Otis moved to cover her as much as possible while the snowballs started striking his back in earnest.

Margaret broke away from him suddenly— and before he knew it, she was pelting handfuls of snow at his sisters.

He could not have been more surprised.

While he'd been protecting her, she had quickly lined up a series of balls unnoticed at their feet but was making very good use of them all now.

Otis hurried to make more, tossing out a few himself but handing most to Margaret. He was used to this sort of behavior from his occasionally brattish siblings, but he'd never expected any lady to want to join in with their usual method of winter warfare.

Margaret had a good arm, and soon it was his sisters' turn to shriek in terror and run and hide behind Mother for protection.

Otis looked up from his kneeling perch to

see Margaret smiling as he'd never seen before. She was blinding, so happy and joyous right now.

Otis felt his attraction to her only increase.

Chapter Seven

Meg stepped from her steaming-hot bath, allowed her maid to wrap her in linen, and began to dry herself off before the blazing fire. Aside from the endless cold, it was easy living here, allowing servants to pamper her and fetch her anything her heart desired. Lady Vyne was emphatic that Meg make herself at home, and Meg had reluctantly agreed to because refusing seemed to make the lady unhappy.

She ducked behind a corner dressing screen to finish her drying off in private. "The weather seems much improved today," she called out.

"Yes, but heavy falls are expected before nightfall," Lady Vyne warned. "Make sure to wear your warmest gown for dinner."

"Yes, my lady."

Meg's new maid handed over thick woolen

stockings that had been warmed by the fire, and then a chemise. To keep the chill at bay, Meg had taken to wearing as many undergarments as possible. It felt a bit constricting at times, but at least she was always warm.

She stepped out from behind the screen to allow the maid to help her into a day gown of burgundy wool and then sat before her mirror. The maid quickly brushed out her long hair and began styling. While she did, Meg observed her hostess. She often caught Lady Vyne frowning and today was no different. Something was on her mind that she would not talk about with Meg.

Lady Vyne drew closer, helping the maid insert a few of her more decorative pins to her hair. "You look lovely."

"Thank you," Meg said, hiding her smile. She felt a bit lovely, too. Despite the cold of The Vynes, she was happy to be here. She had not realized how much she had missed the company of another woman. Even the countess' children's antics appealed to her. The young boy was a sweet little gentleman, happy to perch on her lap occasionally, especially if it meant he was closer to the cakes placed on the tabletop.

The girls were playful, running here and there through the upper floor of the grand house. They were not allowed in any of the ground-floor rooms. Lord Vyne was said to prefer not to see his children more than once a week. Lady Vyne, however, was as devoted a mother as anyone could want.

Because of the absence of affection from their father, all held their older brother, Lord Clement, in the highest regard. He toted them around, played with them, admonishing them to be good or quiet when they became too rowdy. He was a wonderful older brother. He would make a kind husband and father one day too.

She turned away slightly as her face heated a little because she was thinking of him again.

Meg could not seem to forget that Lord Clement had kissed her, but had not tried to do it again since. She was not sure whether to be grateful or despondent about that. He was not avoiding her, but he was busy and always seemed rushed. She rather thought she might like another kiss from him if he was ever so inclined. After all, she was being forced to look for a husband in London. Why not be prepared to pick someone who kissed well? But in order to do that, Meg needed to be able to make a comparison.

"What are our plans for the afternoon?"

"We must wait." Lady Vyne moved to the window, and Meg dismissed the maid. "My husband has invited friends of his to join us for the holiday. They could arrive anytime now, I believe."

Meg was disappointed by the news that she must meet new people. "Who are they?"

"Mr. Xavier Milne. He is a prosperous merchant and quite wealthy, from London."

A prosperous husband might make a good husband too. "I see. Is Mr. Milne married, madam?"

"Indeed he is. His wife has given him several children."

Meg sagged with relief. For a moment, she feared Lady Vyne had invited the gentleman for the sole purpose of meeting her before the season began. Given the secrecy of everything that had gone before to get her here, she would not have been surprised if Hector had arranged something like that. "I do hope they are enjoying a smooth journey."

"Yes, but until they arrive, I am not quite certain how many members of his family will be joining us." Lady Vyne shrugged. "We shall see. Are you ready?"

"Yes." Meg snatched up a woolen shawl and wrapped it about her shoulders.

Lady Vyne smiled and led the way to the door.

They were in the morning room half an hour when a servant came with the news that a carriage was approaching the manor. Lady Vyne seemed displeased by the news but moved to the drawing room to receive them.

Meg was dragged along although she rather hoped she might have been excused. Lord Vyne was already in the drawing room, pacing. Meg had not seen her host more than once since her arrival. He was said to be ill and spent much of his day in bed. However, during the times she had been exposed to his company, she found him a cold and hard man, one with little conversation for Meg.

"I've sent for your son, madam," he said curtly.

Lady Vyne nodded.

Meg looked down at her fingers, feeling ill at ease that any search would be in vain. Lord Clement had left the manor before elevenses. Meg had waved to him from her upper bedchamber window when she'd seen his figure on the snowy lawn below. He'd waved back but continued on his way to the stables. She'd seen him ride off, too, but not return to the manor in the hours since.

"I will expect him to be attentive to all our guests," Lord Vyne informed his wife.

Lady Vyne nodded and arched her neck toward the door. "They are here."

The earl cast a baleful eye upon his wife. "I will speak with the boy later about his absence."

That did not sound very pleasant. Meg eased back as greetings were exchanged with Mr. Milne and a daughter. She seemed about Meg's age but with a polish Meg could never hope to imitate. Miss Milne was spectacularly pretty, with russet-red hair and a heart-shaped face. Meg rather thought she *knew* her looks were superior, too. The pair were very loud and exuberant. Meg did not like them very much.

Miss Milne glanced at Meg, frowning slightly at her presence.

Lady Vyne introduced Meg with a fond smile. "And this is our dear friend, Lady Margaret Stockwick."

"A pleasure, my lady."

"Miss Milne." Meg inclined her head. "I trust your journey was uneventful."

"Indeed it was," she replied, smiling at Lady Vyne.

They all sat down together, and Meg ended up beside Miss Milne. Being new acquaintances in the presence of old friends, Meg held her tongue and let others talk. Miss Milne felt no such compulsion. She added her pennies' worth at every opportunity, drawing all eyes in the room to look at her.

Miss Milne leaned closer suddenly and whispered, "Will Lord Clement be joining us soon do you think?"

"I cannot say," Meg whispered back.

"Have you been visiting long?"

"We arrived several days ago."

"You came with your brother?"

"Indeed. Do you know him?"

"Lord Stockwick and Lord Clement are the most desirable bachelors in all of England." Miss Milne smiled knowingly but Meg couldn't be more surprised about her brother's reputation. Could a man with so little patience be considered a catch?

The gentlemen suddenly excused themselves, announcing they would retire to the library for the afternoon to discuss important business matters. Meg was disappointed to discover that the library would be off limits until they were done. She had hoped to read the next chapter of her book with Lord Clement there upon his return from riding out.

She would have to wait until tomorrow, she supposed.

"It is a pleasure to be invited to stay at The Vynes. My father has been telling me all about the estate and the family's long history here."

"It is my family who once owned this estate but it became part of the Vyne estates upon my marriage." Lady Vyne's smile was strained, and then she gestured to the waiting servant and asked for tea. "Might I enquire after your family? Your mother and sisters are well, I trust?"

"Indeed they are, and very sorry to have missed the opportunity to travel to Derbyshire this year."

Meg leaned forward. "How many siblings are in your family?"

"Eight." Miss Milne eyed the cakes. "There were too many for even the largest of carriages so Papa said they must stay at home with Mama."

"Traveling as a family can be very trying on ones nerves," Lady Vyne remarked.

"Even when you only have the one sibling too," Meg murmured. "Men are so hard to amuse over long distances."

That earned her a laugh from Lady Vyne.

"I should like to have brought my sisters to meet everyone," Miss Milne said.

"It can be difficult to leave home," Lady Vyne replied, eyeing Miss Milne with a more sympathetic expression. "More tea?"

"Yes, please."

Lady Vyne asked Meg the same question but she declined a second cup.

"Cake," she offered next.

Miss Milne nodded quickly and took one slice of cake. Meg declined. She had enjoyed a good meal earlier in the day and needed nothing more.

Miss Milne, however, eyed the last piece

hungrily. "May I have another?"

Lady Vyne agreed.

"Forgive me but I truly am famished," Miss Milne said when it was gone, too. "My father's impatience to reach the estate ensured our stops along the way were always brief."

"Some men never consider the needs of the ladies under their care," Lady Vyne murmured. "My son is not like that."

"No indeed. Lord Clement is very much concerned with everyone's happiness," Meg replied in full agreement.

"I am glad to hear it." Miss Milne nodded quickly.

Meg was not sure why she looked up when she did, but she found Lord Clement standing across the room, still as a post as he listened to her praise him. A funny smile teased his lips, then the smile grew.

Meg's cheeks began to tingle with the heat of a blush.

Lady Vyne and Miss Milne could not see him, and they talked on about the trials of pleasing a large family, with no idea their words were being overheard.

Meg held his gaze and scrunched her toes in her slippers. Lord Clement was finally back, and they might still read her book together that afternoon if he was free to do so.

He raised a finger to his lips, asking for her

silence, and then backed quietly from the room without interrupting his mother.

Meg gaped. Why was he not joining them?

Lady Vyne must have seen something of Meg's disappointment in her expression then, because she whipped around to look behind her. "Is that you, my son?"

But Otis did not reappear, and Meg couldn't even hear his steps on the stairs.

Lady Vyne caught Meg's eye, her expression questioning. "I wonder what is keeping my son away?"

"I cannot imagine, my lady," she murmured.

Lady Vyne's gaze shifted ever so slightly to Miss Milne and a wry smile crossed her face. "I hope whatever it is doesn't keep him from joining us for dinner."

"I cannot imagine it would," Meg reassured her.

Lord Clement had never missed a meal since Meg had arrived. She had enjoyed his company immensely as his conversation had filled the void of emptiness inside her. He had enlivened every meal with his conversation in a way Hector never had. But with the Milnes visiting too, she would not be able to monopolize his time anymore.

Lady Vyne turned to Miss Milne. "Perhaps you'd like to retire to your room to recover from the journey for a short time before we meet again at dinner. If you are still hungry, I can have a tray of tea and sandwiches sent to your room."

Miss Milne beamed. "Thank you, my lady. I would indeed be grateful for some time alone with my thoughts if you can spare me."

Miss Milne left after reassurances were offered. Escorted by her maids and a footman to show her the way upstairs, Miss Milne swept out with a cheerful wave.

"She seems nice," Meg murmured.

Lady Vyne nodded. "One can only hope it lasts."

"Ah, there you are, Mother," Lord Clement exclaimed as he reappeared but at a different doorway than the one he'd used before.

His mother smiled in relief. "We were beginning to worry about you."

"I ventured upstairs to check on the boy. He's doing better I think."

"Did he jump all over you again?"

"Begged to be put on my shoulders and carried around." Lord Clement glanced her way with a smile. "How are you today, Lady Margaret. Warm enough, I trust?"

"Indeed I am."

His mother leaned forward. "I'm afraid you just missed meeting the new visitors."

Lord Clement's eyes widened in apparent surprise, and then he turned to Meg. "What visitors?"

Lady Vyne was only too happy to relate the particulars of the new guests.

"Well, I'm sorry to hear Miss Milne has retired for a while. Damn awful timing really. I was just about to suggest we all take another walk together." He turned to Meg suddenly, brows rising in question.

Meg grinned. "I'd be happy to join you today."

Chapter Eight

Otis rested his feet on the wall in the corner of the library and wet his finger, ready to turn the page. Meg's book was truly terrible but he couldn't rest until he'd caught up with the beginning of the story. He'd sent Lady Margaret a request for the loan of the book so he could catch up late last night, and his valet had delivered it to him at daybreak, before he'd managed to make plans to do anything else.

Beginning a story in the middle had been vastly unsatisfying to him, and he wanted to discuss the whole book with Lady Margaret the next time they met for a reading. Thankfully, he was a quick reader, and he was already a quarter of the way through the story. Unfortunately, his meeting with Meg to read together would be delayed because he was required to spend time with the Milnes that afternoon instead. Father had insisted on being present.

Otis was expected to meet with them at four in this room, resplendent to begin a courtship, but the story was much more interesting than sizing up any woman for marriage.

He lifted his eyes and rested the open book against his chest and gave thanks for Lady Margaret and her unusual choice of reading material. Otis found her utterly charming and far more interesting than Miss Milne. Lady Margaret was quite the surprise really, given the odd remarks Hector had said to her detriment in recent years. Very lively—now that she'd settled into the informal pace of the estate and its occupants. Much more talkative than upon her arrival, too, and spending time with her was no hardship. So entirely kissable that he didn't quite trust himself still.

It was clear that Mother's affection for Lady Margaret was reciprocated, and his siblings begged for her company constantly. Hector would obviously have no trouble finding her a husband once she was comfortable with the idea. She seemed a truly uncomplicated creature. That was a quality quite rare in his experience with women of the *ton*.

"Yes, I think we will all be very comfortable here," a man said suddenly to Otis' right.

"I hope so," a woman replied.

Otis risked a peek as the voices grew louder and louder. No doubt it was the Milnes prowling the house. They were drawing closer to the library and his hiding spot. He could not see them but because he'd left the door slightly ajar, what he soon heard was more than enough for one day.

He closed Meg's book and set it behind him.

"Vyne assures me he'll propose before the week is out," Mr. Milne boasted.

"Yes, Papa," Miss Milne agreed, but to Otis, she did not sound so confident about her chances.

Good.

The library door handle rattled, and then Mr. Milne pushed both doors wide to admit them.

Otis quietly set his feet on the floor. He had been hoping to avoid the Milnes for a little longer but it appeared his luck had run out. Mr. Milne strode to the center of the room and looked about as if he owned the place. "Impressive, isn't it?"

"There are so many books," Miss Milne exclaimed in wonder as she stared up at the walls. "We might finally get my sisters interested in serious matters at last."

"*When* you are mistress here," Mr. Milne

said in a whisper.

Otis rolled his eyes. Presumptive prig! He'd not even spoken to the chit and they were making plans for after the wedding.

"Lord Bellows told me his library was much like this," Miss Milne noted.

Otis' ears pricked up at the mention of Miss Milne's former suitor.

"Not that he could read any of it," Mr. Milne said with a mocking laugh.

Otis was curious to know how Miss Milne considered her former suitor. Bellows was not very bright but he had been clearly besotted with this chit. Otis was certain he had seen affection for the earl when Miss Milne had been with the man.

"He does try very hard," she said briskly. But then Miss Milne turned around and spotted him in his corner. Her eyes widened, and she grasped her father's arm quickly.

Otis stood and tugged down his waistcoat. "Bellows does try extremely hard to hide his difficulties from others. Persistence and loyalty is what he is known best for though."

Miss Milne dipped into a deep curtsy worthy of a court appearance. "Lord Clement," she whispered in an unnaturally reverent tone. "We did not see you there."

"Miss Milne." He took in her appearance and bowed with the appropriate degree of respect for such a woman. This was the daughter he had met before. She was exactly as he remembered, elegant, delicate, somewhat vain, and he felt not a single stirring of attraction toward her still. He would not marry a woman he did not crave to be close to. "Welcome to The Vynes."

"The estate is lovely," Miss Milne gushed. "Your family has been so welcoming."

"I'm sure everyone will have done all that is required to make my father's guests enjoy their stay." He turned his attention on Mr. Milne. "Mr. Milne, I was led to believe that we were not to meet until four. You are somewhat early."

This pair had interrupted his musings about another lady. One he *was* finding himself very drawn to. He wanted them to go away while he considered what to do about Lady Margaret.

Mr. Milne adopted an apologetic expression. "My daughter was eager to see more of the manor. I'm sure you can understand why. Perhaps you would consent to show her around the rest of the house until our meeting."

He couldn't very well claim to be unavailable, so he nodded. "Have you viewed the family gallery?"

"Not yet."

"Please," he gestured toward the door as Mr. Milne hung back, urging him to join them.

There was not a chance in hell he would conduct a private tour of the manor for just Miss Milne. "After you both."

Otis put his hands behind his back as they walked into the hall and turned toward the gallery. More than fifty paintings of unmatched size graced the walls, nestled between tall windows. Given it was snowing again, there was not much to see outside, but in springtime the gallery offered the best views of the garden.

"Oh, these are wonderful."

He pointed toward the wall. "One of my ancestors was prodigiously fond of painting the estate, as you see."

Miss Milne nodded. "Your mother told me your family has lived in this one valley for generations."

"Six generations, on both sides of the family, too. The Vynes and my mother's family, the Morgans, were once sworn enemies."

She smiled. "How was a peace brokered?"

"The usual way. Marriages were arranged between sons and daughters." He shrugged. "Not all unions ensured peace for the newlyweds."

"Yes, I've heard that can happen in arranged matches," Miss Milne murmured with a subtle glance over her shoulder.

Otis glanced behind them, too, and groaned. Mr. Milne was dragging his feet. "Mr.

Milne, I think you will find this painting to your liking."

The man came forward slowly and stopped before a scene depicting a tannery. Milne had started out as an apprentice at such a place, he'd heard, but within twenty years had somehow amassed a fortune that had propelled the Milne family into the heart of the *ton*. "It is an impressive feat to rise from such honest labors. You made your fortune the right way in my opinion."

Mr. Milne colored deeply but Otis was not mocking him. There was no harm in offering the man his respect, given he'd come on a fool's errand.

"What is this one?" Miss Milne asked, pointing to the next painting.

Otis stepped up to it and smiled. "The house before improvements were made by my grandfather. It was quite a bit smaller in those days. This part of the house used to be outside—a walled garden and pond. Of course at this time of year, the pond was often so frozen it was skated upon."

Miss Milne laughed. "Lord Bellows once promised to teach me to skate."

"Surely there is still time for him to do so," he whispered, so her father did not hear the remark.

Miss Milne nodded slowly but her

expression became strained. She flashed a smile that fell far short of sincerity. "Perhaps."

They moved along, and Otis answered every question Miss Milne put to him. He was well schooled in the family history to give the tour, even if he couldn't wait to get back to the book and Lady Margaret. Neither feat could be accomplished until after speaking with his father. But he was impressed by Miss Milne's intelligence. She would do very well for Bellows if Otis could turn her back in the earl's direction.

He glanced at his pocket watch and smiled. "Time to head to the library."

Miss Milne quickly availed herself of his arm. "Thank you," she whispered. "I hope Lord Bellows knows how good a friend you are to him."

"You can tell him, after you marry him," Otis suggested, leaning close. "He tends to get flustered when anyone does him a kindness."

"Well, well, well. This is what I had hoped to see," Mr. Milne exclaimed, grinning widely at the sight of them standing so close together.

Otis untangled himself from Miss Milne. "It's not what it looks like."

"Is it not?" Mr. Milne beamed, and then laid his finger beside his nose. "But I see and hear only that which makes my heart happy."

"We all see what we wish to see in others."

He narrowed his gaze on Mr. Milne. "Did you know Lord Bellows was a good friend of mine before you dragged your daughter here? I could never bear to be the cause of his unhappiness."

Mr. Milne blinked. "She will do her duty."

"Marriage should be based on more than that. Respect. Affection and mutual interests." He caught Miss Milne's eye. "There are no dogs allowed around me. I'm allergic to them."

"Oh." Miss Milne stared. "That is unfortunate."

"Not for me." He gestured them toward the door that led back to the library impatiently. "We should not keep my father waiting longer than necessary. Delays are not good for his health."

He led the way to the library where Father was indeed waiting for them before the fire. Vyne brightened when he saw them arrive together but Otis made sure not to sit too close to the visitors. He would not encourage them to consider a marriage between himself and Miss Milne as a certainty.

It was anything but.

Chapter Nine

Meg took the chair closest to the fire to comb out her long hair, her thoughts fixed on Lord Clement. She had not seen him today but she'd heard he had met with Mr. Milne and his daughter that afternoon. She had hoped to see him at dinner tonight, but he had not appeared. No one seemed able to find him, or Hector either. "I hope nothing terrible has happened to him."

"I'm sure he'll turn up hale and hearty soon," Lady Vyne murmured, apparently unconcerned for the whereabouts of her son. "He has taken a great many responsibilities on his shoulders in recent years. I'm sure he's somewhere on the estate and fully occupied."

"I hope he is warm." The snowfall Lady Vyne had predicted yesterday had settled over them and continued still unabated. Night had fallen long ago, and there was snow piling up thickly on her window ledge. "Lord Vyne is very worried about his absence.

"True, but not for the reason you imagine," Lady Vyne advised.

"I imagine he must miss his son," Meg said.

"Well, you would be wrong," Lady Vyne murmured as she reclined in the opposite cozy chair by the fire, tipping her glass of wine high to drain the contents. The countess' children had long since gone to bed, Miss Milne had retired in a huff, and the gentlemen, Lord Vyne and Mr. Milne, were drinking in the library. Lady Vyne might be a little disguised at the moment. It was just the two of them in Meg's chambers tonight, talking together as usual before they went to bed.

Lady Vyne regarded her gravely as she set the glass aside. "I trust you will keep our family matters to yourself, but you must realize my son and husband are not close."

"Oh, I am sorry to hear that," Meg said quickly. "They have been together so rarely in the same room that I never noticed."

"I'm glad you were spared the tension." Lady Vyne rubbed her brow. "Neither ever hides their true feelings from me."

Meg nodded quickly, worried that to ask more questions would be presumptuous.

"When fathers and sons quarrel, it is always hardest on the mothers."

"Of course, the money now is the source of discord."

"I am sorry to hear Lord Clement is a burden on the estate."

"Money is the least of my son's concerns." Lady Clement frowned at her. "Are you telling me you don't know about the inheritance he received from the late earl, his grandfather?"

Meg shook her head quickly. "Hector tells me very little that is the truth, I've come to realize. I thought Lord Clement's situation must be similar to Hector's, before he inherited my father's estate."

"Their situations were and are vastly different. Otis could afford to buy his own estate tomorrow, one grander than this one, if he chose to ever leave us."

Meg couldn't be more surprised. Otis did not act like he had pots of money. "Why doesn't he? He seems capable."

"He will not leave without us," Lady Vyne admitted, looking away guiltily.

Meg's estimation of Otis' character rose exponentially. He was a good man, more caring than her own brother, perhaps. "You are lucky to have such a son."

"I know."

Meg's comb suddenly caught on a lock of

hair and when she removed it, she discovered a tooth had broken. She held it up, staring at its unhappy state. Since leaving home, it continued to break. She heaved a sigh. "At this rate, I might have to purchase a replacement before Christmas."

Lady Vyne shook her head. "I keep a second new comb laid aside for just such emergencies. I'll fetch it and bring it back to you shortly."

"It is not urgent," Meg protested but Lady Vyne was already out the door, a little unsteady on her feet.

Meg drew her knees up to her chest, made sure her legs were completely under her nightgown for warmth, and stared into the flames. It was comforting being with Lady Vyne, being here in the place she never thought she would ever enjoy herself. These quiet moments at night with another woman offered a companionship sadly lacking in her life since her mother's passing.

And the more she learned about Otis, the more ashamed she became. She had wronged him in her thoughts more times than she could count.

A window rattled suddenly, and a blast of cold air swept through the room, chilling her to the bone.

"What!" she exclaimed, turning towards the window as Otis climbed through it, his shoulders and hair dusted heavily with snow.

He put his finger across his lips to silence her again as he shut it—but then froze as footsteps hurried down the hall in their direction.

His mother's voice rang out, and he suddenly dived under her bed.

Meg bolted for the dressing screen and hastily pulled on her thick winter coat.

Lady Vyne sailed into the room, brandishing a new ivory comb. "I'm afraid I'll not be able to linger with you any longer tonight. I'm needed in the nursery."

"But Lord Clement—"

"Otis will be fine. Do not worry for his welfare so much, my dear," she suggested, and then frowned at Meg. "Were you really going to wear that coat to bed tonight?"

"I was thinking I might," Meg lied. She would wear the coat until Lord Clement left her room.

"I can have a maid deliver another blanket if you like."

A maid might discover Lord Clement. Meg quickly shook her head. "The coat will be enough."

"All right." Lady Vyne chuckled softly. "Well, good night my dear. Sleep well and perhaps dream of hot springs."

As soon as the countess was gone, she

moved to the bed and peered under. Lord Clement was hard to see in the shadows, but she had not imagined his arrival. "You cannot be here," she admonished. "What are you doing?"

"Every window and door downstairs was locked," Otis complained as he slid toward her. "I am very sorry about this."

Meg rushed to the window and looked down. "How did you get to my window?"

"The old vine is still quite sturdy," he answered in a soft voice, and then he glanced toward the door. "I had no idea my mother would be here when I started up."

"We talk together every night."

Otis grinned quickly. "What about?"

"Never you mind," she admonished again. "You had better go."

"True." He started toward the door, but when they both heard voices raised outside the room again, Meg froze and Otis hurtled himself across the bed and threw himself down on the opposite side.

Although impressed by his speed and agility, Meg hurried to the door and opened it a crack. "It is Miss Milne," she whispered to the viscount.

"Do not let her in!" he warned sternly.

Miss Milne and her maid appeared in no hurry to return to their room, though. The pair crept along the hall and, after listening at a closed door, Miss Milne slipped inside. The maid remained in the hall, appearing to be keeping watch.

Meg shut the door and locked it. Miss Milne's behavior disturbed her, but not enough to go out there and ask her what she was doing, creeping into another guest room.

Meg moved to the bed and clasped her hands together before her stomach. "The door is locked now," Meg informed Otis.

He poked his head up and placed his arms upon the bed. He smiled, and Meg was utterly charmed. "Thank you, Margaret," he whispered. "You have saved my life tonight."

"How did I do that?" she asked but felt a little thrill anyway. He was back and obviously well. She had worried for naught about him. But he could have frozen out there. She leaned down and grabbed his coat sleeve, discovering the fabric cold and damp under her fingers. "Oh, you must go to the fire before you catch a chill," she urged, pulling him up off the floor.

He moved slowly to the hearth, where a good fire burned, and sank down on his knees before the flames. He held his hands out and sighed in obvious pleasure. "I'm used to the cold you know, but I dreaded I might have to spend a night in the stables until I saw light at your window."

She nodded slowly and sank down on the nearest chair. "Where have you been?"

"Here and there about the estate. By the way, thank you for not letting Mother know that you saw me tonight, or in the drawing room yesterday."

"How do you know I kept yesterday a secret?"

"Instinct, and the fact that Mother called out my name and I still managed to slip away."

"Why were you hiding from her?"

He added another shovel of coal to the flames. "I do not hide from my mother."

Meg bit her lip. He was clearly not hiding from *her* either, so that just left… "Do you hide from Miss Milne?"

"Yes, but do not tell anyone I said so."

"You do not like her?"

"Not the way I like you." He grinned, and then schooled his features as if he'd not meant to confess that.

Meg couldn't hold back a smile. "She seems quite nice."

"I have nothing against her."

That was faint praise if ever she heard it.

"I had better leave you now," he whispered, as he climbed to his feet and dusted off his coat sleeves.

Meg caught his arm. "Will I see you tomorrow?"

He looked at her sharply. "Do you want to?"

"We were going to read my story together."

"So we were." He nodded. "The library will no doubt be occupied again tomorrow. My father likes to impress visitors with the size of his collection, not that he reads many of them these days. But there is a chamber on the floor above, right above it. The light is good, and no one should think of looking for either of us there. Will you meet me there at four o'clock?"

Lady Vyne took an hour of rest at that time, and Meg thought she could manage to slip away from her maid then, too. "I'll try."

"I'll wait for the hour. Come if you can," he whispered. "It's time to find out what happens next in your book."

Meg nodded…and when Lord Clement leaned down, she allowed him to kiss her again.

It was as lovely as the first time. Lord Clement cupped the back of her head as he peppered kisses over her willing lips. She felt the brush of his tongue across the seam of her lips and she parted them.

Lord Clement devoured her mouth then, and Meg submitted quite willingly. She lifted her hands to his coat and spread her fingers over his chest. A soft moan left her lips, and Otis drew back, blue eyes bright and full of questions.

Meg blushed hotly. "You should go."

He cupped her cheek in the palm of his hand and smiled. "I definitely should."

He crept to the door, turned the key and peered out—and then quickly shut the door again. "Does she *never* stay in her own room?"

"Town hours?" Meg suggested, and then yawned.

"I might have to wait her out." He bit his lip. "I don't want to inconvenience you but might I stay here a little longer? She has to go to her own bed sooner or later."

Meg considered what might happen if he stayed. He might kiss her again, but she did not believe he might try to do more than that. Having him here now already risked her reputation, but if he were seen leaving, and she was in her nightgown, it would be ten times worse. She nodded, knowing there was no other choice but to agree and hope for the best. The alternative, sending him back out the window was impossible. He might freeze. "You may stay."

"Again, you are saving my life," he assured her. "Take yourself to bed and don't mind me."

She glanced at him, and then at the narrow settee. "What are you going to do?"

"Wait by the door and hope I don't freeze. A pity you do not have a spare blanket lying around."

"I have all of them on the bed, but sitting by

the door doesn't sound very comfortable or warm enough for you," she noted.

His brow rose. "Would you have me join you in bed instead?"

Meg gaped. "Otis!"

He chuckled softly. "We could always practice bundling."

"That is a terrible idea." She peeked out the door quickly and grinned. Miss Milne's maid was nowhere in sight and the hall was finally empty.

Otis joined her at the door, and she made room for him. She pushed. "Go."

"Until tomorrow," he said, and then slipped out of the room soundlessly.

Meg closed the door, grinning broadly. She was glad Lord Clement was a gentleman at heart rather than the rogue she'd imagined.

Chapter Ten

Otis flung himself from the carriage in the stable yard of the Lucky Chance Tavern. He glanced around carefully. There were four horses hanging their heads over the stalls inside the stables, one of which he instantly recognized by color and the blaze on its forehead. Lord Hector Stockwick was at the tavern, or nearby perhaps.

He turned toward the coachman. "Make sure the horses are given hay and cover them up while you wait. I'll try not to be too long."

"Yes, my lord."

Otis hurried toward the tavern, brushing snow from his shoulders, flanked by two of the burliest footmen from The Vynes. He'd come prepared for an argument, should Hector not wish to return home with Otis of his own free will.

As much as he'd like his arrival to pass unnoticed, the tavern drew customers from miles around. The taproom was full and loud. He gave the occupants a cursory glance but did not immediately see Hector in their number.

The tavern keeper saw him though and rushed over. "A table and ale, my lord?"

"Not today. I should like to speak with Lord Stockwick if he is here."

The fellow frowned. "I am sorry, my lord. There is no one here by that name."

Hector had a habit of hiding his identity when he was drinking in low places like this, so he would not become a target for thieves. "What about another name? A stranger to these parts. It is a matter of some urgency."

The innkeeper scratched his chin. "There's a fellow abed upstairs, but I never imagined him a friend of yours. He's been malingering here a few days."

The timing sounded right. Otis tried to recall what Hector had worn the last time he been seen. "He might have arrived wearing a blue coat, paler blue waistcoat, and riding boots. He has dark hair and is a little shorter than I. But I swear his horse is in your stable right now, unless he gambled it away."

The innkeeper nodded. "Might be my customer. He owes me money."

Otis sighed and dug in his pocket for coin. He counted out a number until the innkeeper smiled. Otis nodded, hiding his annoyance at the amount. "This is yours if the man upstairs turns out to be my friend."

"I'd be happy to take you to him." The innkeeper led the way, climbing the narrow stairs to an upper floor with a heavy tread. Otis followed, drawing his men with him.

The innkeeper banged on a bright yellow door at the end of the hall and hollered, "You've a visitor."

There was grumble of complaint inside, and Otis recognized the tone as belonging to Meg's brother. "That's him."

Otis handed over the money owed and asked his men to wait outside the door before going in.

He stepped through the doorway and squinted about the dingy little room, noting the décor hadn't improved since the last time he'd been forced to spend the night here due to bad weather. The same faded drapes still hung at the window, unpolished floorboards bare of any rugs graced the floor, and a narrow and untidy bed stood in the center of the room.

A large lump shifted under a faded quilt gracing the bed.

"Wake up, man," Otis demanded. "You've been here long enough."

"Bugger off," Hector complained. "Can't you see I'm busy?"

"Sleeping," Otis noted. "Don't make me drag you out by your heels."

A pair of dainty feet suddenly appeared on one of the pillows. "I think he means it, sir," a woman whispered.

Hector grumbled again and the bedding was flung back from one side. Hector had been sleeping upside down in the bed and, with a bit of effort, crawled out.

Otis averted his eyes from his nakedness. "For God's sake, cover up," he complained.

"S' your own fault for intruding," Hector taunted. "What brings you here so early?"

"It's midday."

"Oh, all right then," Hector agreed then began to look around. He seemed particularly unsteady, and the way he was scrubbing at his head made his hair stand on end even worse than before. "Be a good fellow and help me find my trousers."

Otis moved deeper into the room. He found Hector's discarded clothing scattered all about and a few items worn by a lady. He tossed each piece onto the bed where the woman still hid, saying not a word. Otis cared nothing about the lady, but his friend really should learn to be discreet. "I'll be waiting downstairs. Don't take long unless you'd like my men to truss you like a hog and tie you to the top of my carriage for the return home."

"I'm coming, I'm coming," Hector insisted as he put his trousers on backward. He jerked them back off and tried a second time. "I just need a moment."

Otis glanced at his pocket watch, struggling not to laugh. Hector was a difficult man, more so at this hour. Otis still had a little time to spare, but he was loath to be late today just because Hector couldn't don his trousers the right way round. Meg was expecting him.

The thought of her made him grin.

After last night's encounter and kiss, he was certain he was looking in the right direction for the woman who might be his bride.

"A storm is coming, and I'd like to be home before the roads become treacherous," he announced as he exited the room.

Otis left his men outside Hector's door, with strict instructions to bring Hector within ten minutes, dressed or not. He greeted a few of the locals and he departed the tavern, resisting the urge to linger. He would wait in the carriage.

The air was chilly, and he threw furs over his knees while he waited for Hector to make an appearance. In his head, he rehearsed what he would say to his friend. Asking for Meg's hand in marriage was a delicate business.

He was so close to winning the wager that he could taste the freedom to take his mother anywhere she wanted to go.

Eventually, Hector appeared at the tavern doorway, shading his eyes from the light. He stumbled across the stable yard with Otis' servants helping him along and into the carriage. Hector collapsed on the opposite bench seat with a groan.

Otis wasted no time. "Home," he called loudly as he thumped on the wall.

Hector flinched from the noise. "What is wrong with you?"

Otis studied his friend. He hadn't improved very much since Otis had found him. "Well, I'm not ape-drunk like you are, for one."

Hector pressed a hand to his brow. "I've had a very good time."

"No doubt."

Hector lowered his hand and squinted across the carriage. God, he looked terrible.

"So what's the crisis, man? Why did you come after me?" Hector demanded.

Otis nodded slowly. "My reason for disturbing you is a delicate matter best spoken of quietly. It concerns your sister."

Hector jerked upright. "Is she ill?"

"No, she is very well." He drew in a deep breath before he continued. "I want to speak to you about her future. Taking her to London might not be necessary after all."

Hector groaned. "What has Meg done now? Begged to return home…or wait, has she convinced your mother to let her stay at The Vynes? It is too much to ask for that she might have simply run off with some poor fool and saved me the expense of dowering her at all."

"Your sister has more sense than that, but you might be correct that she is willing to stay at The Vynes." He sighed. "She has asked for you every morning and every night, you know."

"I told you exactly when I would return." Hector's expression turned to alarm. "I'm not late, am I?"

"No. You were expected back tomorrow."

"Good. Then this can wait until tomorrow when my head is clear."

Otis shook his head. "Your clear head is needed at The Vynes now."

"Don't tell me you're lonely without me?"

"No, I have not missed you personally. But Meg does, and there is also Father's unexpected guests, Mr. Milne and his daughter, that you should meet with."

Hector's brows rose high. "How pleasant for you to have so many friends come to call, but I still don't understand?"

"It's Meg."

"You said there was nothing wrong with her." Hector drew close. "Why the urgency to speak of my sister all of a sudden?"

Otis drew a breath, and then wet his lips. "I know this might seem a hasty decision to you…but I wanted to ask for her hand in marriage."

Hector laughed. "Good God, you've a wicked sense of humor. Don't talk nonsense. You and Meg, an ill-matched pair if ever there was one. What is it you really want?"

"Your blessing."

Hector squinted. "But she's hated you for years?"

Otis reeled back. Hate was a very strong word. "That cannot be true."

"Oh, yes. You have no idea how much she disliked the idea of being under the same roof as you for the holiday. We argued about turning back for three days in a row."

Otis shook his head. Meg may have initially believed him responsible for Hector's prolonged stays in London, but he had set her straight days ago. Hector would know her opinion had changed if he'd not been preoccupied with his own amusements at the tavern. "I am convinced she understands now why you stayed away from home for so long. But I am still asking for your approval to court her."

Hector frowned. "Does your sudden change of heart have anything to do with the bet you made with your father? It's all the servants were talking about the day I left."

"What I feel for Meg has nothing at all to do with any wager."

"But in marrying her, you'll win. Why choose Meg over the Milne chit? A large dowry more than makes up for the disappointment of Meg's smaller one."

"The wager is beside the point. So too is the size of a dowry. I care about Meg."

Hector drew closer. "I knew you were desperate to win the wager, but to ask for my sisters hand and claim to love her is beyond the pale."

"I'm not sure it is love, but it is something important. After the last few days of becoming reacquainted, I think she would accept my proposal."

Hector seemed unconvinced still. "Does she know about the wager?"

"No," Otis admitted. "There wasn't time to tell her everything about my family."

Hector shook his head. "You've no chance then. My sister believes in love at first sight and all that romantic gibberish young women go on with. Once she learns about the wager...well, I'm sure you can imagine the likely response. She'll refuse you then, and so do I now. Don't waste your time and energy courting Meg. She was born stubborn."

Otis was not unduly alarmed at being

refused but he definitely did not agree with Hector's opinion of her character. However, had Hector asked for one of his sister's hands in marriage, if they were the right age for marriage, he might have said no too at first. "I wager she won't."

Hector smiled coldly. "Care to put hard coin on that bet."

"I will not buy your approval. Meg's affections are priceless."

"I have told you no, and that is the end of it," Hector insisted. "We all promised to stay well-away from our sisters and if you know what's good for you, you will keep that promise."

"I cannot."

Hector glared, suddenly appearing very clearheaded and angry. "If you so much as touch one hair on her head, I'll throttle you."

Otis scowled. "How will you know what goes on between Meg and I? You're never around her. You make a bloody poor chaperone indeed."

"I will make up for any lapse just as soon as my head clears," Hector insisted.

"Oh good, and when you do, perhaps you could repay me what you owe me. There's the money you took to fund your little excursions to the tavern, to gamble with Moore, or so you said. Then there was more besides that was paid to the innkeeper for your stay. I assume you paid your female companion handsomely for her time, too."

"Of course I pay my way, you penny-pinching prig. I don't know why I bothered coming all this way to be subjected to your disapproval. I had enough of that when my father was alive."

"I hope your father's shade never learns that you abandoned your sister to spend Christmas rutting between a whore's thighs. You should be ashamed of yourself."

Hector's face paled suddenly, and he put his hand up to his mouth. "Stop the bloody carriage."

By the time Otis stepped out, Hector was hunched over and casting up his accounts with painful persistence. Otis watched in silence, but then when he was done and appeared weak, he strode over and helped Hector into the carriage.

"My thanks," Hector murmured as Otis tossed every blanket over him. "You are a true friend in my hour of need. I don't feel at all well. Let's forget we ever quarreled."

Otis shook his head, no longer amused. "I do this knowing Meg would want me to look after you as if you were part of my family already. You don't deserve an ounce of pity."

His complaint was met with a loud snore.

Chapter Eleven

$\mathcal{M}$eg wandered The Vynes with a sense of anticipation building inside her. Casting an eye upon every clock as she moved from room to room, she checked the time to be certain that she would not be late for her meeting with Lord Clement at four. Meg had not seen him since last night, but that was not unusual. He was frequently busy about the estate, or he was with his younger siblings, doting on them.

She would never have believed Lord Clement a family man if she had not seen his good and steady influence on the children with her own eyes.

She stepped into another room, finding herself in the family gallery again. Of all the paintings hung upon the walls, she found the summer landscapes the most pleasing. This valley was so beautiful when bursting with green rather than smothered in white.

It was very possible that she just might see that transformation with her own eyes soon, if she had not misunderstood the intent behind Otis' exciting kisses.

Something had changed between her and the viscount last night. Developed beyond superficial curiosity about each other. She thought perhaps that Otis might be sincerely interested in her as a woman. One he might be willing to court if things continued to go well between them.

Meg was definitely interested in Otis, and not just because encouraging him might spare her from being dragged to London for the season. She had not been looking for a husband here, but she wondered if she might have stumbled upon one. She did not like to think Otis would bestow his affections in the hope of getting under her skirts. He would not do that to a friend's sister. She believed he had very honorable intentions toward her.

"Ah, there you are, my dear,' Lady Vyne cried as she burst into the gallery hall. "I've been looking for you everywhere."

"Here I am," she promised with a smile. One day, all going well, Lady Vyne might be family, a mother figure perhaps who she could count on for advice. "I was just walking about for the exercise."

"Miss Milne is doing the same, except upstairs."

There was not very much to see in the upstairs halls, unless one slipped into bedchambers that were not their own, as Miss Milne was wont to do. Meg preferred the lower rooms and the views to be found rather than snooping about. "Are the children still at their lessons?"

"I expect so," Lady Vyne said as she fell into step beside Meg. "Did you give any thought to my question of the other night?"

"Which one?" Meg asked, smiling. She honestly couldn't remember ever being asked so many questions about her likes and dislikes. The countess had questioned her thoroughly in the past few days. There were so many decisions she would have to make before she was fit to move about in society. Dresses, slippers, parasols, colors. If she married Otis, she might be spared most of that chore. He had claimed he spent most of his time here in Derbyshire with his family, and so would his wife, too. But he also moved in society a few weeks a year. Meg would have to navigate that world if her husband wished her to.

Lady Vyne moved so they could see each other. "I asked what sort of husband would do for you, young lady," she complained. "You said you would let me know, and yet I am still waiting. Well?"

Meg laughed softly and thought of Otis. "Someone I can admire."

"Someone handsome and important?"

"Kind at heart, and a gentleman who could make my toes curl in my slippers when we are together."

Lady Vyne laughed. "Ah, to be young and able to discover love anew. I envy you, and Otis too, in some respects. It is such a time of confusion and wonder. I do wish you all the best in your search for your husband, Meg. All your mother wanted for you was to be happy, and I aim to make that come true."

"I'll do my best to choose wisely," Meg promised, picturing Otis at her side as they spoke their vows.

Lady Vyne frowned suddenly as she looked about them. "I should have asked Miss Milne to join us, but I truly wish it could be us alone for a while. One grows so tired of being questioned constantly."

Meg's curiosity stirred. "Questioned? What about?"

"My absent son. Would that Otis had already chosen his bride."

She considered the countess, and what she might say if she learned Otis had stolen three kisses. Would she be happy? "What sort of woman do you wish your son to marry?"

"Someone that I like as much as I like you, but I will not hold my breath," the countess mused. "I just hope she is someone who understands the importance of family. You've seen how Otis is with his siblings. He treats them as if they were his own children rather than brother and sisters."

"I did notice he had some," Meg grinned impishly, "managing tendencies when they were around."

"He's very protective of all of us," Lady Vyne protested. "And that is exactly what you must have in your husband. You need someone you can depend upon."

Yes, a protective husband would be an advantage, but only if they valued her opinion, too. "I begin to wonder if my brother will ever marry."

"He will one day. As for my son, it is highly likely he'll marry Miss Milne before the season even begins."

Meg gasped, unable to hide her shock at that announcement. Otis couldn't marry that vain creature! And he had kissed Meg...but was that all it could be? "I had no idea he was courting her."

Lady Vyne raised a brow. "This is my husband's doing. Since his health has declined, he's become obsessed with Otis' situation. He invited the Milnes to ensure the match."

Meg wet her lips, her stomach clenching with disappointment. "So your husband wants Otis to wed."

"My husband expects a proposal to be made before Christmas Day arrives."

"I see." She looked around quickly, making sure they were still alone. "What does Otis—I mean, Lord Clement want?"

"He told me he intends to marry soon, and I believe him sincere."

"I understand." Meg nodded.

She could make Otis happy, if given the chance. She might even have become accustomed to being half frozen all the time just to please him, too. "He should marry someone who makes him happy," Meg murmured.

"I hope so, because when you marry without love it is an unending torment."

Meg looked at the countess quickly. She was slowly coming to understand that all was not as it seemed in this family. The earl and countess did not act as if they loved each other. Meg had assumed the pair were like her parents. Forever holding hands, making decisions together. Lord Vyne seemed disinterested in spending any time with his wife or his children. "Not everyone finds love," she suggested.

The countess' skin grew pink. "No,

sometimes they throw their chance away to win a ridiculous wager," she bit out savagely.

Meg did not like how that sounded or the countess' apparent outrage, and didn't dare ask what she meant.

But Lady Vyne noticed her anxiety. "Can you believe my foolish son made a wager with his father to marry before the season even begins? I predict he will be made unhappy by any alliance made under those circumstances."

Lady Vyne caught her by the shoulder when she stepped back in shock. "I cannot believe he would do such a thing."

"Oh, don't worry, my dear girl. It will all be over soon enough, I expect. But never think I won't love you best. We will still write to each other, and one day when things have settled, I shall have you visit The Vynes again."

Any hopes Meg might have harbored in her heart of a mistake withered and died. No alliance made in haste, because of a bargain or an indiscretion, ever turns out well in the long run.

She stared at the nearby landscape and her heart tore in her chest. She could never return to The Vynes when Lord Clement was married. That would be too painful. She had foolishly fallen for him.

Lord Clement was not the man she'd imagined him to be, and she should have been more cautious about exposing her heart to a near stranger. However, in a way, she should be grateful to him. He had reminded her what it felt like to feel desirable and part of a larger group. He'd also taught her a valuable lesson—a rogue was a rogue, no matter how distinguished in name. Since her brother planned to launch her into society soon, she was sure she needed that clarity in the coming months as she assessed the gentlemen she was introduced to.

"Lady Vyne," Miss Milne called out suddenly. "Lady Vyne, are you there?"

The countess groaned softly and turned, smiling as her other guest appeared in the doorway. "Yes, Miss Milne."

"Oh, Lady Margaret. I did not see you," Miss Milne exclaimed with a silly giggle that made Meg cringe.

Miss Milne was wearing an exquisite gown of silk and lace that looked much too light for the drafts and chills of the manor. Meg glanced down at herself, realizing that there was no competing with such a well-turned-out creature. She didn't even want to try.

Miss Milne clapped her hands together. "I was thinking we might all take a walk out of doors together. I haven't yet seen the stables, and I would like to ride in the spring."

"Unfortunately, I must meet with my

housekeeper," Lady Vyne said, her voice tinged with regret. "Perhaps it could wait until tomorrow."

"What of you, Lady Margaret. Will you walk outdoors with me?"

Lady Vyne laughed softly. "Coaxing our Meg out of doors when it is snowing would be quite an achievement."

Meg shrugged. "I don't care for snow."

"Then I think you must have visited at the worst time of year," Miss Milne exclaimed. "You simply must come back to visit in the summer, when it's warmer. The grounds are lovely then."

"I wasn't aware you had visited the estate before?"

"Oh, no. But I was talking with Lord Clement the other day, right in this very spot, and he described everything so well I have become enraptured. When he speaks, I can imagine the sights and scents of this beautiful place as if it were my home, too."

Meg shivered. "He has a pleasant speaking voice."

Meg had come to feel at home at The Vynes, too, because of Lord Clement's warm welcome, but she'd been utterly mistaken that he might have had any honorable intentions toward her. She rubbed her brow. "Would you excuse me, my lady? I think I have taken a chill."

Lady Vyne rushed toward her but Meg backed away. "I'm sure its nothing that a night in a warm bed cannot rectify. I am sure I will be fine in a few days."

Lady Vyne's face fell. "I'll send up your maid."

"I'd rather you didn't."

"How silly to refuse your maid," Miss Milne said. "Who else will plump your pillows?"

Meg had managed quite well without a personal maid before, and there was no reason she could not do so again. "I'm just going to lie down and hope for sleep."

"I'll send up a tray with some tea and broth later," Lady Vyne decided. "Our housekeeper herself will attend you. I absolutely insist."

"I don't want to be a bother," Meg murmured. "If my brother should return tonight, would you let him know that I need to speak to him about London tomorrow? Tell him…I've had a change of heart."

Lady Vyne's eyes narrowed on her. "I'll do that as soon as I see him," she promised.

"I do hope you feel better soon, Lady Margaret," Miss Milne called. "I would hate you to miss the joy of the holiday. You never know what might come yet!"

A wedding—but not one she could look forward to.

"I'll ring when I wake, when I'm hungry, and if I am not better by morning, I'll summon your housekeeper." Meg backed away.

As soon as she was clear of the room, Meg rushed upstairs to hide in her bedchamber for the night.

Chapter Twelve

Otis crooked his finger at the maid to draw her toward his bedchamber door. "Well?"

"She *says* she's ill, my lord," the maid confessed.

"Is she?"

The maid glanced away. "I couldn't say, my lord."

Otis slumped back against the wall, wondering why Meg Stockwick would ever feel the need to pretend ill health. Mother said it came upon her suddenly, and he was concerned enough to send spies into her room to check on her welfare.

When the hour to meet with Meg to read together had come and gone with no sight of her, Otis had gone in search of Hector, thinking they might be together. But Hector was huddled in bed, claiming he was about to die, which was far from true.

Otis had sent his valet to care for Hector and then approached Mother, who passed along the message that Meg was so ill, she would not be joining them for dinner that night. He had endured dinner with his parents and the Milnes' company in a distracted state and fled as soon as he could.

He glanced at the maid again. "Did Lady Margaret ask for a tray to be sent to her room?"

"Yes, my lord, but she barely ate any of it."

Concerned, Otis looked down the hallway toward her distant bedchamber. He wanted to speak to Meg, to find out for himself how she fared, very much. "Does she know her brother has returned?"

"Not that I know of. She never asked about him."

Otis nodded. It was likely Hector would be recovering for a few days like the last time he'd overindulged. It was a blessing that Meg would never know just how bad he got at times. "Thank you, you may go."

The maid bobbed a curtsy. "Yes, my lord."

When the maid was gone down the servants' staircase, he stepped back into the hall and closed the door on his room. He was probably expected to return downstairs soon to join the Milnes and his parents, but he could not. His heart was not willing to wait another minute to see Meg.

He put her book under arm and, aiming for nonchalance, sauntered down the hall. When he was level with Meg's door, he stopped, knocked and ducked inside quickly.

Meg was curled up under a blanket by the fire, sniffling into a gentleman's handkerchief.

Her eyes widened at seeing him in her room again. "You shouldn't be here."

Despite the impropriety, he hurried across the room and fell to his knees. "I was worried about you."

"There's no need to concern yourself with me," she said, drawing back from him

He smiled quickly and pressed his hand to her cheek and then her brow. "There is when you feel unwell. At least you don't appear fevered."

She moved her face out of reach. "Shouldn't you be with your family and guests?"

"The Milnes can wait," he said as he sat back on his heels. Meg's eyes were a bit red, and so was her nose, but otherwise, aside from a little sniff now and then, she seemed well enough to his eye. "It was a quiet dinner without you tonight."

"Was Miss Milne not entertainment enough?"

"She might have been if I could pay

attention."

Meg's expression hardened. "Is that how you will be with her?"

"Probably. If she expected more, she should have married Lord Bellows last year when he was courting her."

"Obviously she found him lacking," Meg insisted. "Is he another rogue?"

"Bellows? Hardly. And denying that you love someone just because they are not smart enough to please your family is a mark against her in my book." He frowned. "Why are we talking about Miss Milne when it's you I want to hear about?"

"We are talking about Miss Milne because you are going to marry her."

"No, I'm not!"

Meg frowned. "Your mother told me you were."

"Then she is very wrong."

Meg's eyes narrowed on him. "Was she wrong about the wager too?"

"Ah, no." He raked a hand through his hair. "I was going to mention that."

"How could you have made a wager to marry Miss Milne and then kiss *me*? Your family and hers expect a proposal!"

"I made a wager with my father to be married within three months. I never specified *who* I would propose to because I did not know at that time. My plan all along was to find someone who I can talk to, worry about, and have them feel the same about me. I think I've found her at last."

"I see," she said, looking ill at ease.

"Rediscovered her." He grinned. Did she really not know she'd captured all of his attention? His heart too. Perhaps he'd have to be more obvious about his interest in her. "As to the timing of any marriage to meet the terms of the wager, I thought three months would be long enough for you to decide to accept me or not."

Her brow furrowed. "Accept you?"

He swallowed down his anxiety. Since he was already kneeling, he freed Meg's hand from the smothering warmth of her many blankets and held it. "My dear Margaret."

"Meg," she murmured.

"My dearest Meg then." He took a steadying breath. "We barely know each other but the moment I saw you, I think I knew my heart would be yours."

Meg gaped. "You want to marry *me*?"

He nodded. "Very much."

"I don't know what to say," Meg said as her eyes widened even more. "Why me?"

"Why not you? I ordinarily don't go around kissing intelligent, funny and stunningly beautiful women all the time or stealing away to read her favorite book together." He produced her copy and laid it on her lap. "There are a few more chapters in this one still, but The Vynes library is vast and largely unread. Or we could purchase our own books together after."

"After you win the wager?"

"Yes. I don't want to leave my mother and siblings behind."

"You expect me to live here?"

"Not necessarily. If we did marry, I hoped we could spend the summer by the sea and have my mother and siblings join us there, too. The warmer air would be better for you and my little brother." Since an agreement seemed a long way off, he shrugged. "I only ask that you consider me. Take as much time as you need to decide one way or the other. In the meantime, I have brought your brother back to the estate since you've missed him so much."

"You left the estate to get him for me?"

"A short jaunt to the village tavern. While I was with your brother, I did ask his permission to court you. He refused."

"On what grounds?"

"Pigheadedness, most likely." Otis winced. "And he was a cup shot at the time. I did not perhaps choose the best moment to broach the subject. I am hoping he will reconsider. I am prepared to wait and ask your brother again and again, until he changes his mind."

Meg bit her lip. "No, don't do that."

"Meg, I must have his permission…or is *no* your answer?"

Meg suddenly smiled. "It is my birthday next month."

"I did know it fell not long into the New Year. But you won't be here then. You'll be in London getting ready to be courted by dozens of bachelors with very good taste in women. You'll be lured to dark corners and kissed by other men."

"I find that highly unlikely. I never wanted to go to London. I'll be one and twenty on this birthday, and you know what that means."

"You'll not need his permission to marry anyone soon!" Otis sat forward and gripped her hand tightly. "Hector led me to believe you were a year younger!"

"Hector never remembers my age. He always forgets my birthday, too, and that has been a blessing when it came to discussions about the future. If he had realized my real age, he might have been even more desperate to marry me off."

"I'm glad he has not." He kissed the back of her hand. "Will you think about it and let me know."

"Yes," she promised.

Otis nodded. "Thank you. I hope you feel

better soon."

"Good news has a way of healing the worst hurts. Otis, that was *the* yes!" Meg leaned forward, and suddenly her lips were pressed against his.

Otis groaned and pulled her closer. That wasn't easy because she was bundled up all warm and snug. He couldn't get close enough for his liking, so he moved some of the blankets aside and slid under them to sit at her side.

Meg laughed softly and wrapped her arms about his neck and held him tightly. "I was so upset to imagine I might never kiss you again."

"Did you pretend to be ill because you thought I would marry Miss Milne?"

Meg's face turned pink and she looked away. "Miss Milne is everything I'm not."

Otis cupped her cheek, his heart bursting with joy. Meg really did care about him. "She's in love with a friend of mine, not that she will admit it."

Meg silenced him with her lips. Otis didn't want to hear another word about Miss Milne, either. She was happy, and Otis was happy, too. She drew back slowly, drinking in the stirring look in his eye. "I like this," she said softly. "Being with you. Kissing you."

"I can tell," he teased, and then brought his lips to her cheek. "There's nothing better for me, either."

He moved along her jaw, peppering her skin with tiny kisses. Meg tilted her head and invited him to continue. Otis did, and she shivered.

He chuckled softly. "Do you want me to stop so you can huddle back under your blankets? I should probably go. We can discuss what we do next tomorrow."

"Don't go yet," she whispered. "I want you to myself for as long as possible. When everyone learns we intend to marry, we might never be alone until our wedding day. I need a few more kisses from you."

Meg kissed him again with flattering enthusiasm. As Otis wrapped his hands around her waist and lifted her closer, almost onto his lap, he was breathless with anticipation. He began to caress her body, and she did the same, spreading her hands over his shoulders, touching his face as they kissed. Soon she had wriggled fully onto his lap.

She even pushed back some of the blankets to get closer.

Otis slowly lowered one hand down her side and then farther along her leg. His touch was light, careful. He desired her but he would not rush her into making love to him.

Meg suddenly covered his hand with her own. "I like it when you touch me."

He nuzzled her neck. "I could continue if

you lifted your hand."

She lifted it, and that was all the proof he needed that his attentions were welcomed.

His slid his fingers softly over her ankle and thick stockings. As he moved his hand under the edge of her nightgown, skimming her woolen stockings until he reached bare skin, she gasped and writhed delightfully.

He pressed his lips to her brow and then caught her face in his hand. "I shouldn't take liberties. Not until our wedding night."

"What if I think I've been a spinster long enough? Would you believe me wanton if I admit to being very curious about the pleasures to be found in the marriage bed?"

"Never." His brows rose. "Such a boon would be more than I deserve."

She grinned back at him. "I've heard that ladies enjoy intimacies. I desperately wish to know if that's true."

He tightened his grip on her head. "You'll enjoy everything about our life together, I swear it."

Meg got up from the settee and held out her hand to him. "Show me."

Otis was on his feet in a second and swept her up into his arms to carry her across the room. When they reached the bed, he pulled back the covers and placed her atop the sheet gently then kicked off his shoes and untied his cravat before joining her.

Meg pulled him down on top of her, a little nervous laugh escaping her lips until he kissed her. He settled on the bed at her side as they continued, exploring each other with their hands. Meg pressed her body into Otis, anticipation thrumming through him.

He lifted her nightgown slowly, caressing her thighs as it rose higher.

When his fingers slid into her curls and he touched her intimately, she moaned and parted her legs wider.

Otis delved between her folds, touching her in a way that could only bring her pleasure. She held on to his shoulders and started to rock against his fingers.

He liked that she displayed no hesitation or doubt. She could not still her body, as she writhed against him constantly. He slid his fingers lower and found her damp core. Moving as slow as he could, he slipped his fingers into her tight channel. She seemed not the least bit worried that he was taking her innocence. She was enjoying what they did far too much for doubt.

"Otis," she whispered desperately.

"Soon, darling, let me tease you a little longer."

Otis teased his fingers into her again and again, biding his time. He wanted to see her give herself over to pleasure. He ached to feel her around him too.

Otis drew back to loosen the buttons on his trousers and drag his shirt over his head. When he moved closer to Meg, she threaded her fingers in his hair and kissed him again. "You. Are. So. Warm," she noted between kisses.

"So that's why you like me so much?"

"That and a few other things," she promised.

Her fingers slid down his bare back, a little cold, and he shivered. "Such as?"

Meg stilled and then her fingers slid beneath the waistband of his trousers at the small of his back. She pressed him tighter against her lower body. Another moan escaped her lips. "That is one."

Otis brushed his erection against her sex more firmly, and then he brought them closer together as he shoved his trousers out of the way.

She gasped as he eased into her body, and her grip tightened on his backside even more as he started moving inside her.

He leaned his brow against hers as they rocked together. It felt so good. Almost too good. He would not last. Otis slipped his fingers between them and teased her clit. She stiffened suddenly, and then she cried out.

Otis quickly covered her mouth with his lips

to stifle the sound, and a few moments later he groaned, his body jerking as he found his own release too.

They gasped for air and slowly parted.

Firelight danced over the ceiling above them and Meg whispered, "That was lovely."

"Indeed," Otis said as he drew Meg against his side. She burrowed closer to his warmth as he drew a deep calming breath. He was going to marry Meg and he couldn't be happier. He nuzzled her hair—content and replete. "The perfume you wear reminds me of the summer I spent at your home as a boy. As intoxicating as making love to you."

"I could never imagine being so happy," she responded.

"Neither could I, until you. Are you warm enough?"

"Yes," she whispered. "Very warm with you beside me."

He nuzzled her neck. "May I stay a little longer?"

"Yes, Otis," she whispered, and then laughed. "You are the most remarkable bed warmer I've ever had."

"Happy to be of service," he whispered. "I'll warm your bed every night if you want me to."

For an answer, she pulled him close and kissed him again.

Chapter Thirteen

$\mathcal{M}$eg was in the portrait gallery the following morning, bundled up from head to toe in her thickest coat, wool scarf and felt cap to keep the ever-present chill at bay, when Otis strolled up to her. She had been alone, waiting for breakfast to be served in a nearby room, and Otis wasted no time in pulling her into his arms, tilting her backward, and kissing her witless.

When he allowed her to rise, his cheeks were flushed and his eyes were bright. "Good morning, Meg. Merry Christmas."

"Merry Christmas," she answered, blushing hotly. She patted his broad chest, still astonished by the way she felt when he held her close. "I trust you slept well."

"I didn't even try," he told her, slipping an

arm around her shoulders. He drew her along to the far end of the long room. "Someone very particular was on my mind this morning."

"Who could that have been?"

He stopped and cupped her face. "The woman I think I might love." Meg blushed as he kissed her again, but he drew back too soon. "I have something I want to give you."

From his pocket he produced a small silver case.

She turned it over in her hands, completely baffled. "What is it?"

"Something I think you might find invaluable in the coming years when you are cold."

Meg carefully opened it and found, not jewels, but matches.

She started laughing as she removed one slender, sulfur-tipped match. "A priceless gift for me." But Meg felt bad. "I have nothing to give you. Hector did not give me time to make or purchase anything for someone like you."

"Having you say yes to me is enough of a present for this year," he promised. He kissed her cheek, and then sighed. "I have to talk to Hector today. Set things in motion."

"Ah, yes, Hector," she said, and then pulled a face. "If he puts in an appearance."

"Oh, he certainly will show himself this morning." Otis grinned. "I snuck into his room earlier, laid out his clothes, put his fire out and opened a window to let the winter in. I'm sure he'll be downstairs and complaining at any moment that he is starving."

Meg laughed. "Why didn't I think of that?"

Otis squeezed her to his side. "You're not as cruel as I am to him."

Perhaps that is what had been wrong with her life all along. She had tried to look after her brother and he clearly didn't want to be coddled by her. "Are you sure we're not rushing into this?"

Otis grew quiet but then he grinned. "We probably have rushed things a little, but I don't believe I will regret anything about us. Are you having doubts now?"

"Not really. But I am a little worried about you, and what your father will say? He's not going to be happy that you're going against his wishes."

"One problem at a time," he suggested as he squeezed her shoulder again.

Otis had fully explained the wager, shown her proof that there was no particular bride included in the bet. He was free to marry anyone he chose and would win if they married within three months. After last night, Meg had little incentive to delay the marriage. She'd chosen Otis to be her husband when they'd shared her bed last night, and liked what they did together too. And there was the anticipation, unexpressed, that she might soon be carrying Otis' child. Meg desperately wanted to make a family of her own with Otis.

When they reached the doorway to the breakfast room, everything was ready. Otis bid her enter first. Otis' siblings were squabbling over which chairs they would sit on but Otis drew her to the other end of the room and held out a chair. "You take your tea with milk, don't you?"

"Yes, I..." She looked at him in surprise. "You take yours the same."

He winked. "I noticed that, too."

The London newssheet from last week was on the table near them and Otis offered it to her first. "Not today, but thank you for asking."

When Otis moved to the sideboard and loaded up two plates, Meg sighed a little. Christmas had always been her favorite season and now she had even more reason to love it. Otis would make a very attentive husband. He made her so happy already.

They talked quietly for most of the meal but then Hector arrived. He seemed grossly put out, not to mention unwell. Puffy eyed and pale, he squinted at the food as he loaded a plate for himself. When he sank into the opposite chair and groaned, Meg considered her chances of engaging in a reasonable conversation with him were slim.

So she ignored her brother, ate well, and chatted with Otis, relishing the small seemingly random brushes of his arm against hers. Eventually, the children left the room and it was just the three of them enjoying breakfast together.

She glanced across at her brother and then drew in a deep breath. She really wanted to marry Otis but she had to have her brother's permission first.

Otis spoke before Meg could think of a way to start that conversation. "Are you feeling better now?"

Hector scowled at him. "I'm fine."

"Good," Otis said. "Perhaps we might continue our conversation from yesterday."

Hector's scowl only deepened, never a good sign. "What conversation?"

"The one we were having before you cast up your accounts beside my carriage?"

Meg gasped. "You never told me he was ill."

"It is the sort of illness that only time can cure." He chuckled softly, settling his hand lightly over hers. "More tea?"

"Yes, please," Meg murmured, deciding not to press for particulars. She didn't want to drive her brother away. At least, not until he agreed to let her marry Otis. After that, she might not mind ever seeing him again. He didn't exactly inspire her loyalty.

Otis refilled his cup too. "I haven't changed my mind. I want to marry her."

"To win a bloody wager," Hector exclaimed, throwing her a warning look. "Can you believe this?"

Meg felt Otis' touch on her back. She grinned slowly, even wriggled back against him. "I know all about the wager, Hector, and I think he's been very clever. When he wins, he'll take his mother and siblings on a holiday. Somewhere much warmer I hope."

"Definitely somewhere warmer," Otis promised.

Otis' father entered the room. This was the first time Meg had seen him in the morning room at this hour. Lord Vyne seemed a bit pale and a servant hurried to seat him and serve him.

Once he had a plate of food before him he dismissed the servant and looked across at Otis. "You will accompany the Milne's into town and show them around."

"I'm afraid that is impossible," Otis replied. "I have other plans today."

"What other plans could you have more important than engaging in a courtship?" Lord Vyne nodded. "Milne is expecting you to be attentive to his daughter."

Meg sucked in a shocked breath that Lord

Vyne would speak so boldly of such a matter while she and her brother was still in the room.

She glanced first at Otis and then at her brother. Surely Hector would prefer Otis to marry someone he really wanted and not Lord Vyne's choice.

Otis caught up her fingers and held her hand under the table. "I cannot do that."

Hector slowly lowered his fork down, his gaze speculative on Meg and then his gaze dipped a little. He shook his head and a smile appeared. "Hmm, yes I suppose we do have quite a lot to talk about today. Lord Vyne, Lord Clement has asked for my sister's hand in marriage and I am giving them my blessing. We have yet to decide the wedding date."

Meg couldn't contain her smile, and tears formed in her eyes. Hector would let her marry Otis after all. She wanted to hug him, thank him, but she didn't want to let go of Otis' hand quite yet.

Lord Vyne gaped. "What?"

"He asked quite boldly too. Would not take no for an answer." Hector offered her a smile. "I guess that means it was love at first, or is it second, sight."

Lord Vyne suddenly smiled. "Well, well, well. So you've finally given up. I'll have the carriage brought around immediately."

Otis' grip tightened on Meg's hand.

"Whatever for?"

"The terms of our wager were very clear." Lord Vyne seemed positively smug. "If I win, you leave."

"Those were indeed the terms but I have not lost or conceded you the victory. I was to begin a courtship and marry within three months. Stockwick has approved my suit and has agreed to a wedding as soon as possible."

Lord Vyne's eyes narrowed. "But you chose the wrong woman, my son. No offence intended Lady Margaret."

"None taken," Meg murmured.

Otis threw a smile her way. "Oh, I definitely chose the right woman to be my wife. I chose with my heart. The terms of our wager did not specify the lady I must wed. Perhaps if you read the wager again more closely you will see I am right. It says nothing about who I would marry just that I must."

The earl shot to his feet and stormed out.

The silence in his wake was deafening. Otis raised Meg's hand to his lips and kissed her. "That went better than I expected. Thank you for your timely intervention, Stockwick. I promise my mother will be much more enthusiastic about our news than my father just was."

"We should go and tell her the happy news soon. I'd rather Lady Vyne hear it from us than from your father." Meg glanced at her brother who was watching her through squinted eyes.

Hector was nodding slowly. "So that's that?"

Meg blushed. "You *did* want me to marry."

Hector grunted. "Now if only I could be rid of the estate as easily."

Otis stood. He pulled Meg to her feet and led them both toward the drawing room. "I actually wanted to talk to you about that, Stockwick. I think I may have a solution that makes perfect sense for both of us."

Hector glanced up at a bunch of mistletoe hanging over the threshold of the drawing room now and sidled around it. "Really?"

"Obviously we cannot stay here year round. It's much too cold for Meg."

"I will stay if you wanted me to," Meg promised Otis but then she noticed the drawing room had changed. "Oh my."

She moved away from Otis and her brother. There was a tree almost reaching as high as the ceiling in one corner, decorated with ornaments hanging from the branches. Something she'd heard royalty did, but she'd never seen it done before. Other things were far more familiar and brought a smile to her lips. A Yule log burned in the great hearth and although night was a long way off, the mantle blazed with a dozen or more candles. It was an enchanting scene that reminded her so much of Christmas' past.

"I thought I might purchase your estate and make a home there for our family," Otis was saying.

Meg spun around to stare at him in astonishment. "Really?"

He nodded quickly. "I knew the first day I saw you again that I would do anything to make you happy. But there is a benefit to me too. I want to see the estate prosper again."

Meg bit her lip and stared at her brother. "You truly don't want to live there do you?"

"Not for even one more night." He nodded slowly and then held out his hand. "We can discuss your purchase of the estate tomorrow when we begin to draw up the marriage contract."

Meg laughed as the deal was struck. "This is the happiest holiday of my life."

Hector cleared his throat loudly. "I don't hear a *thank you, Hector*?"

"Thank you," she cried. Meg rushed to her brother and gave him a quick hug then threw herself into Otis' waiting arms. "I've never been happier to be so wrong. This is the best Christmas ever."

Epilogue

Meg hurried down the stairs of The Vynes, mortified that she had overslept on the most important day in her life. At her side was the woman who would be her mother as soon as the ceremony concluded. Her brother was pacing at the bottom of the stairs.

He looked up scowling. "What time do you call this?" he complained.

"Every woman is entitled to be a little late for her own wedding," Lady Vyne argued. "Now say something nice, Hector, or don't say another word."

Hector wisely buttoned his lips shut.

The countess seemed the only person he ever listened to, especially about the wedding. She faced Meg and teased another two tendrils of hair free to frame her face. "Your mother would be so proud if she could see you today. If she were here, she'd say there had never been a lovelier bride."

"Thank you," she whispered, fighting back tears. She still missed her mother desperately, but having the countess standing in for her made the pain of loss lessen. She impulsively kissed her cheek. "Thank you for all you have done to make today so special."

"You've done more for me than you'll ever know, too."

Lady Vyne was coming with them to Dorset and taking her children with her for a long holiday. After a brief argument between the couple, and a few threats of locked doors and cold dinners, the earl had relented to uphold his end of the wager as long as she promised to return. Lady Vyne had agreed but not stated when that day might be. She had learned a little something from her son's example.

"You'll have a wonderful holiday with us," Meg promised. "Are you packed and ready to go?"

The countess nodded quickly. "And very keen to see a new horizon and a new home."

Lady Vyne hurried into the drawing room with a little wave. Left just with Hector now, Meg smiled brightly. After today, she did not know when she would see her brother again. He was headed to London to enjoy life as a bachelor with no responsibilities whatsoever. She tugged on his sleeve. "You were right all along. I never knew what good would come of taking this holiday. I should have thanked you before now, but I am grateful that you brought me here. I've had a wonderful Christmas."

"I didn't expect you to marry him when I wrote to the countess." Hector nodded. "But now that you are about to marry, I can say I am glad to be spared the expense of a London season."

Meg punched his shoulder. "Miser."

"I'll have you know I intended to spoil you terribly," he admitted. "To make up for Mother and Father not being with us anymore, I was prepared to spend a fortune on clothes and carriages so you would feel you belonged. The best shops to patronize are in London, my dear."

"I don't need to be spoiled to feel loved. I don't think you know how happy Otis makes me." A shadow passed over Meg, and she shivered. "Oh, the drafts in this place."

She was quite done with the cold and snow that forever shrouded this valley in mist, at least for this year. She might have to live here when Otis inherited this estate upon his father's death, but she hoped that was a long way off.

He pressed a kiss to her brow suddenly, and then held out his arm. "Come along, sister dear, your betrothed awaits his beautiful bride. Probably most impatiently, too."

Pleased by Hector's behavior, Meg slipped her arm through her brother's.

Hector walked her steadily toward Otis but all she wanted to do was run into his arms. As she took her place beside her betrothed, a shiver raced over her skin again. She stumbled through her vows in a state of acute excitement. When the ceremony was over, and she had taken her husband's name, Hector approached her again, but Meg's eyes were drawn to a shimmer of light beside him.

For a moment, she could swear her parents were staring back at her...and then the shimmer was gone.

Meg shivered.

Otis wrapped his arms about her. "Have you become cold again, my love?"

She turned to look up at her husband's grinning face and realized he'd not seen anything amiss. "A little, but I was just thinking of my parents and wishing they could have been with us."

"Who says they were not?" He kissed her cheek and then her lips. "Spirits have been known to haunt The Vynes. There have actually been several sightings in the library. Maybe your parents took their own holiday here to keep an eye on you."

Meg laughed at the idea but hoped that if it were possible, they had. If so, then her father would know how the book ended, and that Meg and Otis' story was just beginning. She couldn't wait for what happened next.

Desire by Design

A surprising offer...

Spinster Sylvia Hillcrest will never marry, but that does not mean she has to ignore the occasional flirtation aimed her way, or the chance to indulge her secret vice in societies best card rooms. When she's suddenly given a fortune to wager, but asked to lose it to one particular family, it's an intriguing challenge too irresistible to pass up. So too is the devilish marquess carelessly flirting with her every chance he gets.

...a secret delight

Faced with a situation he cannot solve alone, the Marquess of Wharton designs a masterful scheme to use Miss Hillcrest to pass a small fortune to a desperate friend. His plan, of course, was destined to succeed, and he spends one scandalous night celebrating with the spinster in his bed. They agreed it was just a fling, but what's a marquess to do when he craves so much more? Is it possible he's finally met his match...or will her secretive ways tear them apart?

More Regency Romance from Heather Boyd...

DISTINGUISHED ROGUES SERIES
Book 1: Chills
Book 2: Broken
Book 3: Charity

Book 4: An Accidental Affair
Book 5: Keepsake
Book 6: An Improper Proposal

Book 7: Reason to Wed
Book 8: The Trouble with Love
Book 9: Married by Moonlight

Book 10: Lord of Sin
Book 11: The Duke's Heart
Book 12: Romancing the Earl

Book 13: One Enchanted Christmas
Book 14: Desire by Design

WILD RANDALLS SERIES
Book 1: Engaging the Enemy
Book 2: Forsaking the Prize
Book 3: Guarding the Spoils
Book 4: Hunting the Hero

SAINTS AND SINNERS SERIES
Book 1: The Duke and I
Book 2: A Gentleman's Vow
Book 3: An Earl of Her Own

REBEL HEARTS SERIES
Book 1: The Wedding Affair
Book 2: An Affair of Honor
Book 3: The Christmas Affair
Book 4: An Affair so Right

MISS MAYHEM SERIES
Book 1: Miss Watson's First Scandal
Book 2: Miss George's Second Chance
Book 3: Miss Radley's Third Dare
Book 4: Miss Merton's Last Hope

And many more…

About Heather Boyd

USA Today Bestselling Author Heather Boyd believes every character she creates deserves their own happily-ever-after—no matter how much trouble she puts them through. With that goal in mind, she writes steamy romances that skirt the boundaries of propriety to keep readers enthralled until the wee hours of the morning. Heather has published over 40 regency romance novels and shorter works full of daring seductions and distinguished rogues. She lives north of Sydney, Australia, with her trio of rogues and pair of four-legged overlords.

You can find details of her writing at
www.Heather-Boyd.com

www.ingramcontent.com/pod-product-compliance
Lightning Source LLC
Chambersburg PA
CBHW050537190726
48284CB00003B/1116